Many
Mansions

ISABEL BOLTON

DOVER PUBLICATIONS, INC.
Mineola, New York

Bibliographical Note

This Dover edition, first published in 2020, is an unabridged republication of the work originally published by Charles Scribner's Sons, New York, in 1952.

Library of Congress Cataloging-in-Publication Data

Names: Bolton, Isabel, 1883–1975, author.
Title: Many mansions / Isabel Bolton.
Description: Dover edition. | Mineola, NY : Dover Publications, Inc., 2020. | Originally printed: 1952. | Summary: "Isabel Bolton, an acclaimed National Book Award finalist, tells the spellbinding tale of Margaret Sylvester. She is in her eighties, lives alone in a New York hotel room, and decides, after considerable deliberation, to reread an unpublished manuscript about her life. Her poignant and sometimes tragic story is communicated with astonishing brevity and immediacy"— Provided by publisher.
Identifiers: LCCN 2019041809 | ISBN 9780486843414 (trade paperback) | ISBN 0486843416 (trade paperback)
Classification: LCC PS3525.I553 M36 2020 | DDC 813/.52—dc23
LC record available at https://lccn.loc.gov/2019041809

Manufactured in the United States by LSC Communications
84341601
www.doverpublications.com

2 4 6 8 10 9 7 5 3 1

2020

Many
Mansions

BOOK 1

ONE

It had snowed in the night, but the snow had been removed from the streets. It rained. The asphalt shone black and glistened in the rain, the tops of the taxis glistened, the umbrellas of the pedestrians and the rubber coat of the policeman at the corner of Twenty-eight Street gave off a bright metallic sheen. The air heavy with clouds and smoke and rain hung like a shroud over the city. In the tall office buildings clustered at the foot of Madison Avenue the lights shining in the assembled windows gave the effect of countless diminished suns and moons peering dead and rayless into the gloom and diffused an ominous light like the amber glow that fills the atmosphere before a summer storm.

A radio in the next room blared out the news, from the clouds above came the purr and drone of an airplane and from below the noises of the streets; motor cars grinding their brakes, tooting their horns; sirens, an ambulance, in the distance the louder siren screech of fire engines. In another room a telephone rang insistently. Wires under the pavements, cables under the seas, voices upon the air weaving the plots, weaving the calamities, thought Miss Sylvester, beating her breast in that dramatic way she had.

She was a small creature with delicate bones and transparent parchmentlike skin and her fragility lent her the appearance both of youthfulness and extreme old age. Her face under its crown of perfectly white hair was illumined and animated by cavernous dark eyes that seemed in the most striking manner to isolate her spirit from the visible decay of her body and in the play of her expression there was that immediacy of the countenance to respond to the movements of the heart which is always so noticeable in the faces of children.

Living so much alone she was in the habit of talking aloud— interrupting her thoughts—"My God, it cannot be! Preposterous. Impossible." Old age was very obstreperous indeed and life perched up here in her sky parlor amid these congregations of lighted windows, looking into all these offices, watching people sitting at desks, at telephones, dictating letters, plowing through the most monotonous tasks, was bleak enough in all conscience and with this welter of imponderable event flowing through her mind, "Good God," she frequently asked herself, "Who am I? What am I? And what's the meaning of it all, these people—all this business conducted high in air—listening to these hotel radios, these telephones and this roar coming up from the streets as though escaped from the infernal circles?" After all, she was human; she had her human needs. Caged up like this!

But now the protest and revolt that had lighted her face went suddenly blank and was replaced by gentle, reminiscent expressions, for she had had an extraordinarily beautiful experience in the night—the nights of the old were stranger than strange. She had waked from a dreadful dream, sobbing, still, it seemed to her, violently shaking her grandmother and when she had subdued the sobs she'd lain trying to orient herself. She had touched, or imagined that she had done so, the edge of the bureau, her hand had knocked, or she'd thought she'd knocked it against the wall; the wall retreated while the doors and the single window of her room were replaced by other windows, other walls and doors, and she had had the most bewildering sense of knowing and at the same time not having the slightest idea where she was, listening to many voices while large vistas—lawns and trees and meadows and blue skies and oceans—opened up to her and people appeared and disappeared in all the various rooms through which she searched. Gradually she made out that she was in her own small bed which she had been sure was on the left of the window now restored to its proper position. Left was left and right was right. And there she was correctly located in space while a clock struck twelve. She'd counted the strokes and crossed a threshold. For it was, she'd remembered, her birthday, the first of February 1950, and if she could believe such a thing she was now eighty-four years old. Highly awake to the inordinate strangeness of it all she'd crossed her hands upon her breast aware that gratitude was streaming from her heart. Gratitude, she might very well demand, for what? Just for this—being alive, feeling the breath plunging up and down beneath her hands—her life, this river on which she had been launched, still warm, still continuing to flow. She knew quite well that her hold on it was most precarious—she frequently prayed to be severed from it altogether, and moreover, she realized that life was not likely to offer her change or variety, here she was cooped up in her small room in this treeless iron city. Nonetheless she had her memories. The Kingdom of Heaven was within her. For after all what kind of a heaven could anyone conceive without these images of earth—these days and winds and weathers? Estimated by human events she would not have said that her life had been particularly fortunate. There had been plenty of catastrophe. She had had to bear for many years an intolerable secret which she would carry with her to the grave. However, what did these personal tragedies matter when measured up against a moment like this—fully conscious of carrying in her heart the burden and the mystery, filled with awe and wonder and rejoicing in that warm shaft of living breath plunging up and down beneath her hands?

Her condition had been a free gift. She had done nothing to induce it. There she had lain consumed with wonder, awe and reverence. What a comfort it had been to feel warm and without pain. The room must have been at just the proper temperature. The blankets felt so soft, the mattress so extremely comfortable. It had been a pleasure to luxuriate in flesh and bones that were not for the moment racked with pain.

The life of the aged was a constant maneuvering to appease and assuage the poor decrepit body. Why, most of the time she was nothing more than a nurse attending to its every need. As for the greater part of the nights one's position was positively disreputable—all alone and clothed in ugly withering flesh—fully conscious of the ugliness, the ignominy—having to wait upon oneself with such menial devotion—Here now, if you think you've got to get up mind you don't fall, put on the slippers, don't trip on the rug. There now, apply the lotions carefully, they'll ease the pain; that's it, rub them in thoroughly. Now get back to bed before you're chilled. Here, take the shawl, wrap it round your shoulders. Turn on the electric heater. It won't be long before you're off to sleep. Try not to fret and for heaven's sake don't indulge in self-pity. This is the portion of the old—having to lie here filled with cramps and rheums and agues—so aged and ugly with your teeth in water in the tumbler by your bed and your white hair streaming on the pillow and the old mind filled with scattered thoughts and memories, flying here, flying there, like bats in a cracked old belfry—haunted by fears, visited by macabre dreams.

Dear me, dear me, she thought, looking through the gloom into the lighted offices, if she could meet death upon her own terms how often she would choose to die. How beautiful to have floated away upon that tide of reverence. It was one's ignorance of just how and where death might come to take one off that made it hard to contemplate. There were all the grisly speculations.

Would she have a stroke followed by a helpless dotage? Would she die of some grave heart condition long drawn out? She might be run over any day by a taxi or a truck. She might slip on the sidewalk and break a leg or a femur. She could hear the clanging bells, the siren of the ambulance that gave her right of way, bearing her off amid the city traffic to the nearest hospital. She could see the doctors and the nurses going through their paces—everything efficient, ordered, utterly inhuman—all the nightmare apparatus attendant on keeping the breath of life in her another day—who knew? Maybe another week; maybe a month or two longer—the oxygen ranks and the transfusions, the injections—penicillin and the sulfa drugs—Heaven knew what! And would there be sufficient funds she wondered to pay for all this nonsense—keeping the breath of life in one old woman more than prepared to give up the fight? Expenses mounted to the skies. Nurses were worth their weight in gold. And as for private rooms in hospitals! All these extravagances. Dear me, dear me. Could she imagine herself in an Old Ladies Home—in a hospital ward?

She worried woefully about her finances. Eating into her principal like a rat eating into the cheese, the only capital that remained to her those few government bonds. However, she'd figured it all out very carefully. She could live to be ninety—selling out a bond when necessary and keeping something for emergencies. Was it possible that she'd live to be ninety?

Not likely at all; most improbable!

And if she did, she'd have to take the consequences. She had always been a fool with money. She knew nothing about the care of it. When she thought about the foolish things she'd done—the naive way she'd listened to all those charming philanthropic young men who knew so well how to advise the single and unguided! It made her sick at heart. But the one decision she had made—capricious, unadvised—to settle on that unborn child a gift of seventy thousand dollars she wasted not a moment's time regretting. After the completion of those arrangements if she'd had any sense she should have put her money into an annuity. They were, she supposed, fool proof. She was glad, however, she hadn't done so (she did some swift and inaccurate sums in arithmetic). She wouldn't be very much better off than she was now, and not a cent to leave to anyone. Those bonds, that balance at the bank could be bequeathed.

What a great lift, for instance, it would give to Adam Stone—how surprised he'd be, how grateful if she were to die tomorrow, to find himself heir to all she had! Poor Adam, she thought, poor Adam! And why not? Wasn't he after all the only person in her life today for whom she felt genuine concern? What if she had picked him up in a restaurant? What if she had known him only a few years? Why not?

He was in his peculiar way as much of a solitary as she was herself—an odd, unhappy, interesting young man. He seemed to stand for her as a kind of terrifying symbol, seeing behind him many similar youths who had played their part in the great war and had returned without zest or hope or faith in life. And why would it not be so—marked and marred as they had been with the impact of the dreadful years? When she talked with Adam she seemed to feel the presence of a crowd of witnesses, all the young in every corner of the world. Against his bitterness, his utter disrespect for life, what was there she could say? She imagined that in his queer way he rather liked to feed upon his bitterness. You could not disagree with him; he resented argument. He would not brook contradiction. There was something rather superb about his anger—working it all out as far as she could see in a kind of sullen passion for art, music, literature. Books he devoured ravenously. He was, she gathered from his conversation, at work upon a novel. He had cast off his family. He had cast off one girl after another, or very likely one girl after another had cast him off. There was something hard, passionate and scrupulously scientific about the way he went in for these brief affairs of love—a short interval of violent passion followed by a tremendous battle of the egos—bitter, sensual, with neither romance nor beauty, but nonetheless rewarding because of some necessity he seemed to feel to further document his vast accumulating dossier on sex, all without doubt to go into the novel he was, if not at present, some day bound to write. He seemed to be driven from one sterile episode into another.

Poor boy, she thought, poor Adam. Was she justified she wondered—"A young man you met in an Armenian restaurant," she said leaving the window and going to her desk where examining her check book and still continuing to talk aloud she muttered, "yes yes, taking that twenty-five thousand dollars that still remains to me in government bonds and adding my deposit, let me see, let me see, $3,497 and some odd cents, there would be in all (she added up the two figures) exactly $28,497.26."

A tidy little sum. She supposed the proper people to think about were the poor old women of her acquaintance scratching along on almost nothing. She knew a number of them—there were several right here in this hotel, unutterably dreary, desolate and brave. How wonderful for one of them to wake up some fine morning and find herself heir to twenty-eight thousand four hundred and ninety-seven dollars and twenty-six cents.

But the rub was of course how much of this would still remain when she was dead. The uncertain residue—she had practically made up her mind to it in the early hours of the morning—should go to Adam Stone. The weather prevented her from going, as she had resolved to go this very day, to Maiden Lane to see old Breckenridge.

But then there were other things that she could do and as she was thinking so seriously of also bequeathing him her precious manuscript, she really should before she determined to do so sit down quietly and read it from beginning to end. What a strange thing it was she thought as she went into the bathroom to attend to the preparation of breakfast, finishing it, laying it away, never able to reread it. And why did she feel so urged to leave it in the hands of this peculiar difficult young man? What was it that consumed her—this hunger in her heart? And was not the most astonishing experience just this—old age? When all was weariness and pain and effort, when the chief business of every day was waiting on her body like a patient old nurse waiting on an unwilling absentminded child, to feel this fierce preoccupation! Was it because she had wanted to call in her conscience—her soul, her memory, as you might call in a priest at the last moment to offer absolution, that she had undertaken the writing of this book?

Well, well now at any rate she must put her mind on breakfast—this smuggling in, hiding away, pretending you didn't make a kitchen out of your bathroom and a refrigerator out of your window ledge was a technique she'd mastered to perfection, she thought, stooping to fish a saucepan and an electric plate from under the bathtub, filling the former with water and attaching the cord of the latter—putting the water on to boil, opening the window to bring in butter, cream, fruit. She flattered herself she pulled it all off pretty well. It wasn't that she didn't grasp as eagerly as a child whatever pleasures life still offered her, there was something even a little sly about her manner of enjoying her small gratuitous blessings, as though she'd stolen a toy from the attentive nurse who kept watch over her or cake and candy from the august angel into whose hands old Nanny might at any moment deliver her. She made it her business to make as much out of her days as her frail margin of health allowed, lunching or dining at a restaurant and, what with the sandwiches, the yogurt, all the queer food that you could find in little tins, managing somehow to sustain herself. There was something a bit miraculous about her little feats and arrangements.

It took fortitude she admitted. The old deserved to be commended for their gallantry. Goodness, when she thought of the necessary chores—putting clothes upon their backs, food into their mouths, getting on and off the busses and across the roaring streets. Courage, self-assertion, vanity were all required. As for herself how ridiculously vain she was—always shaking off the kind and attentive people ready to assist her, as though to say, "Thank you very much indeed, I'm quite capable of looking after myself," still trying to look as though her appearance suggested youth and vitality, never able to forget that she'd been, and not so very long ago, an agreeable and attractive woman. She was capable, she acknowledged it, of the most absurd behavior—little coquetries, high and mighty airs.

But maybe she could be forgiven for believing that she had in her eighty-odd years of life accumulated a little sagacity. She had her insights and divinations. Did she not carry all the seasons in her breast? All the ages of man were hers; and if she liked to watch the great human comedy with an impersonal yet highly sensitive and inquisitive eye, that was certainly her prerogative. If she was always skipping out of her own skin into the skin of somebody else was it not her way of editing her own experience to which she'd gained at her age a perfect right? Innocent and innocuous she might appear as she sat eating her lunch or her dinner and generally engaged in saying to herself—"Oh, yes, my dear lady, my dear gentleman, you may not be aware of it, but I know practically everything there is to know about you." It wasn't that she gave herself up entirely to staring. She enjoyed her food enormously. Her luncheon or her dinner out was the great event around which she planned her entire day. But she hoped and prayed she would never resemble the positively ghoulish old ladies she often observed addressing their plates as though the only passion that still remained to them was the appeasing of their hunger. How their table manners, their bright and greedy eyes betrayed them! She ate, she hoped, with restraint and circumspection. If she sometimes allowed herself a cocktail or a small bottle of wine it was with the belief that it sharpened her perceptions. She liked to lay herself open to every breeze of insight and divination.

The old were in it as well as the young! Plenty of old ladies. They got about in the most gallant fashion—joined up in the macabre procession; birds of a peculiar feather. One saw them everywhere with their permanent waves, their little hats set on their heads at such rakish and ridiculous angles, their coats and shoes and handbags following the prevailing fashion, tottering in and out of shops and restaurants. How avid and excited they appeared as though they wished to let you know they had their own important engagements to meet like anybody else. Life seemed to jostle and push the poor old things around; pretty exposed they somehow were. The family offered them no shelter or asylum. If they had sons or daughters or great-nephews or grandchildren they did not share their homes and even if they had been invited to do so would the independent old things have accepted such an invitation? Where were they housed? How did they manage it all? The restaurants were full of them. What with the vitamins and the excitement, the movies, and the radio, the prevailing atmosphere of carnival and cocktail bar, the buffeting and the exposure didn't seem to kill them off.

It was, she remembered, under the influence of a dry martini—sipping it alone in the Armenian place on Fourth Avenue that she had picked up poor Adam Stone. There he'd sat buried in his book, his sullen, rather beautiful face looking extremely self-conscious. And why not? For he was, she had discovered, perusing Dante's Inferno. What a pity, she had thought, that she was not young and charming, for she could read Italian too and this might have been one of those daydreams in which she guessed the young man beguiled his lonely condition come delightfully to life. "I see you're reading Dante," she had said; and when he'd taken in the situation—her ancient face together with the dry martini—he'd been quite naturally as rude as possible. However, she'd persisted. She had her ways with young men; she was not without intelligence.

They had entered into conversation. Every time they had met they had continued to converse. And now, although he would not for the world admit this was the case, she helped very substantially in mitigating the solitude that overtook him in his all too frequent girl-less intervals.

Poor Adam, she reflected, examining her tray to make sure the breakfast she had now prepared was properly assembled; she'd not seen him for several months—he'd as likely as not found himself another girl and more than probably moved to a new address.

It occurred to her as she carried the tray into the bedroom, seating herself at the desk, that she would not be able to tell Mr. Breckenridge where to get in touch with him in the event of her demise. To think of making a young man her heir whose address she did not even know. Dear me, dear me, the anonymity of people's lives.

Anonymous was the word for everyone—anonymous. Why, the precious self was shattered, blown to bits a thousand times a day and it was actually the case that there was something of insolence, a kind of effrontery about it if anyone presumed to have an assured assertive self—opinions, a personality of one's own. It was incumbent on us all to do so many turns and tricks in adapting to thoughts, ideas, events, that if one showed oneself incapable of this agility of heart and mind there was a very real danger of lapsing into indifference, lack of sympathy, imagination, as though the poor battered soul were ready to lie down and say I'm beaten, numbed, dead, finished. Listening to all the assorted information, the nerves supplied with the new, the necessary antennae, the soul destroyed by the vibrations; why, the wholesale, the unprecedented calamities of the world cried out to us, shouted aloud every minute of the day. Yet who among us could endure to listen?

It was too much, too much for anyone she said, thinking as she spoke of her poor Adam. Poor boy, he held out against it all so stubbornly. He was without any knowledge of love; he did not, it seemed to her, understand the meaning of pity. He simply held out against letting it get him down. Such wholesale calamity diminished, dwarfed his little private griefs—the personal grievances and tragedies to which she guessed he clung tenaciously. It was for this reason she imagined he was so obsessed with sex. Out of his curious affairs he got but little joy, unless you could account the strife, the bitter conflict of two egos in their uneasy and anonymous roles attempting to assert their own authority, a kind of cruel self-inflicted pleasure.

Yes, Adam clung to his dwarfed uneasy self. You might say it had burrowed down in him, gone underground and as a witness of this there was that novel she was so sure that he was writing—a queer backhanded method of reasserting, reestablishing his dignity, authority. Goodness, think of all the lonely anonymous men and women there were today attempting to do the same thing; why, the novels came off the presses as fast as leaves in autumn falling from the trees and a novel was no matter what its subject matter as authentic a way of telling the tale of self as any that could be thought out.

Hadn't she, an old old woman sat down and tried for seven whole years to thrust into novelistic form the story of her life? And why, she'd like to ask herself had she when it was finished locked it up in that desk drawer and never had the nerve to look at it again? And why now did she have this strong desire to place it in the hands of Adam Stone? Vanity was certainly involved. Adam would have to revise many of his notions about her. She'd have to admit that the idea amused her. Moreover he would, she imagined, discover that it had literary merit. She somehow felt it had. He'd take it in all probability to a publisher and after she was gone it would doubtless see the light of day.

But beyond all this there was a deeper reason. Didn't she long to convey to him more intimately than she'd been able to in conversation something that she had realized in their talks together he'd not only held out against but found completely phony—her capacity for reverence, wonder, of which there was in his own constitution not a trace.

Not a trace, she said, rising with some difficulty to her feet. And was it not about to be extinguished in the human heart? Consternation, though few people would be able to recognize that this was so, standing out as we all somehow did against it, had usurped its place.

We simply stood aghast, she thought, crossing the room to get the morning paper which she must read before settling down with her manuscript (yes she was now firmly resolved to read it from beginning to end). "An excellent day for such a resolution," she said, opening the door, taking in the *Times* and returning with it to her desk.

Pouring herself a second cup of coffee she sat down and spread the paper on her lap. The headlines sprang at her—the nightmare world in which we lived—all these chimerical events through which we passed. "Impossible, impossible," she cried—"it staggers the imagination." But here in large black letters was the announcement—Truman Orders Hydrogen Bomb Built—a fact at the disposal of everyone capable of reading. Within a few hours it would be lodged in the hearts and minds of most of the inhabitants of earth—hundreds of millions of people would quail before it as she was quailing now.

But who could really comprehend the cryptic data at the core of it? The words were Greek to her as they would be to all but a meager handful of her fellow mortals—concepts of the mind, mathematical measurements, calculations of inconceivable complexity. They affected her in some odd way as though she were reading poetry; the syllables fell so sonorously upon the ear.

> "Molecules composed of two deuterons and a proton.
> Two tritons, a deuteron and a proton,
> A triton and a proton and a proton and a deuteron.
> In one of these six possible combinations—
> Triton—triton, triton—deuteron, triton—proton,
> Or a possible combination of these three
> Lies the secret of the triton bomb."

You'd have to possess the brain of Einstein to understand it.

But here it was—the perfidious, the majestic secret explained if you could get it, and the words dancing with such terrible agility in her mind and heart.

> "The triton bomb
>   is the last step
> In a six-step process
> One taking more
> Than six million years."

Could it be possible? Could it be humanly possible that the diligent, the honorable search for truth, the inquiry into the secrets of nature and the structure of the Universe would be closed and consummated with this annihilating explanation?

"The protons are hooked on,
    one by one,
    To an atom of carbon
Two of the protons
Losing the positive electron
    And are thus transmuted
    Into an electron—
As has been seen
    A nucleus of one proton
    And two deuterons
    Is a proton nucleus
    This is by far
    The most powerful reaction
    In nature
    And takes place
    In the sun
    At the rate
    Of four pounds an hour
    A reaction time
    That brings it within
    The range of possibility."

The paper dropped from her hands. She threw back her head and closed her eyes. "What is man that Thou art mindful of him or the son of man that Thou visitest him," she cried aloud.

TWO

Patsy had come down to the sidewalk with him. She shivered for she was clothed only in her slacks, a light sweater, and a pair of huaraches. "There's the precious manuscript," she said, placing a well-stuffed folder in the laden pushcart that stood against the curb. Adam took it angrily from where it lay exposed to wind and rain, and repacking it with great solicitude in a nest of similar folders, turned to speak to her. But she'd gone without so much as saying goodbye. He could see her through the open door of the tenement house fleeing up the stairs to her own little flat on the third floor. To be sure, she'd offered to go along with him, and help him unpack his things. But he'd turned her down flat. "No, you don't, my little bitch," he'd said—the word had escaped him. There had been something in the way he'd said it that had, he expected, as good as terminated the whole affair.

He resented the note of sarcasm with which she referred to his manuscript. He was done with Patsy. He surveyed the cart on which his goods and chattels were now untidily stowed away. The sight of the familiar objects was discouraging enough. How many times they'd gone with him from one place to another. A reproduction of van Gogh's *Old Shoes* peeped at him from behind an alarm clock, and a portion of Picasso's *Clowns* emerged from his old trench coat. God, how many books. There was his old victrola with a crank to wind up the turntable and a few albums of fine records. His radio was wrapped in a blanket. How had he ever managed to acquire these possessions, to move them from one place to another?

The desolation that invaded him for the moment swallowed up his wrath. The sheer discomfort of digging into new quarters, unpacking and placing his books, setting up a table for his typewriter, rigging up some kind of contraption where he could cook, accustoming himself to the unfamiliar chairs, the unfamiliar bed, the general disorder and despair. A rut he could endure, but to meet with new contingencies—that's what got him down. It was Patsy who had found the room; she had even offered to go along with him and help him settle in. "But no you don't," he said grimly, starting to push his cart through Jones Street into Bleecker, "no, you don't, my little bitch," and at this moment, turning east on Bleecker, a flight of pigeons wheeling all together and catching on their tilted wings some diffusion of brightness from the breaking clouds seemed to illuminate not only the dark skies but the murk and drabness of the February day. They gleamed and disappeared behind the belfry of Our Lady of Pompeii, just as Adam, all but knocked down by a heavy truck, and answering with peculiar vehemence the curses of the driver who had forced him and his pushcart against the curb, experienced an extraordinary instant. Half a dozen or more doors opening in his heart while he passed through as many moments in memory, and an accumulation of loneliness, a quite unutterable sense of his uniqueness flooding the present instant, brought him so intense a consciousness of all he'd learned of misery, despair and solitude that he seemed to have acquired nothing short of spiritual treasure. Hounded by misfortune, accustomed by some ill star that pursued him to the kicks and bludgeonings of fate, he would grind out of the misery and torture a work of art; he'd wrench a masterpiece from all that life had meted out to him. So, turned back upon himself—for he was a young man, he felt, quite sure of genius—ravenously devouring his experience and his bitterness, brushing the mud from several books that had been jostled from the cart, continuing his virulent exchange of curses and obscenities with the driver of the truck, he received so vivid and immediate a sense of his own predicament, all the vicissitudes of his late affair with Patsy, that, scrapping half the material of his novel now in progress, he determined that he would place the first big chapter of his book right here, in this very moment—Bleecker Street, with the low ramshackle houses, the dormer windows, the tenements, the pushcarts, the fruit and vegetable stands, the Italian vendors, women marketing, children and baby carriages, the street cries, the mud and drizzle. He'd make you smell and see and hear and live with it. And in the midst of the animated scene, he'd place himself, a young man with his goods and chattels in a pushcart, shoved up against the curbing while these profanities came pouring fresh from the wells of his misery and anger—getting square with Patsy, getting square with life.

The traffic jam broke up, the trucks rolled on. Seeing an opportunity to cross the street, Adam maneuvered his cart to the opposite curbing and looking up saw the pigeons flying in close formation emerge from the clouds a second time and wheel behind the belfry and the golden cross. God, he'd snare those pigeons too, shedding their light from the cloud just like the Holy Ghost descending on the Village, and he'd introduce that newsstand there between the pushcarts with the morning papers and the headlines in English and Italian, shouting out their joyous message—the great big beautiful news about the great big beautiful bomb, the absolute weapon to blow the human race to Kingdom Come.

As he nipped into Morton Street, pushing his cart in the direction of Seventh Avenue, the truck driver's abuse and his own foul-mouthed rejoinders mingling with the rhythms of the headlines, "Truman Orders Hydrogen Bomb Built," still visualizing pigeons and pushcarts, fruits and vegetables, the belfry and the golden cross, and seeing as though he stood before him in the flesh Philip Ropes, with his chestnut-colored curls, that Byronic throat, the collar open at the neck, and remembering Patsy naked on her bed, her delicate fragile body white as a camellia, the soft red pubic hair, the red curls exquisite beneath her arms, he seized upon the plight of the planet with a kind of ungodly glee—(just another item to throw into that magnificent chapter). He'd feed that chapter all he had—this first day of February 1950—H Day, Hell Day, Hydrogen Bomb Day, call it what you like; but it was this sweet, the acute, bitter business of the individual life that mattered. Making scenes, drawing pictures, holding imaginary conversations, he saw a series of astounding chapters, his entire novel unfolding as he marched along.

It would not be a shallow, just a surface novel. He'd throw one value up against another. He'd experienced plenty—plenty. And here for some reason or another, Mol got trammeled up in the big rush of his memories and reflections—My Old Lady—Mol—poor intense emotional Miss Sylvester. He could see her now with her big eyes and her highfalutin talk. He knew just how she'd agonize about it. It couldn't be—it simply couldn't be. The great mistake, the greatest mistake in history, Mol opined, the using of the bomb at Hiroshima. How she'd gone on about it—protesting so violently, unable to see how anyone could disagree with her. Well, if she'd marched through France or Flanders and seen those hundreds of bombers in their ordered flight moving morning after morning with spectacular promptitude into the sky—roaring like a thousand trains of cars into her field of vision and out again, on their way to Berlin, to Dresden, to Nuremberg, to murder the mothers and the babies and the children and the old people—to destroy the factories and the railroads, to soften up the job for the artillery—if she'd thrown her hat in air and cheered them day after day till the breath was drawn clean from her lungs, she might be ready to shrug her shoulders now, and say, what's the difference—a thousand bombers, or one bomber with the one big beautiful bomb—what did it matter?

Here he was, at any rate, on this first of February, in his lone and penniless condition, with the check on Philip Ropes the third, which he had intended to tear up but which as a matter of fact reposed in his pocket at the present moment fairly burning a hole in his pants.

Philip Ropes the third, for Christ's sake—he hauled up at Seventh Avenue and waited for the lights to change—there was actually no reason why he shouldn't cash that check. Patsy owed him the money. And if she'd paid him with a check on Philip Ropes, why be so stiff about it? The whole blamed business was over between them. Let Patsy go and do Ropes's typing. Miss Patricia Smith— Typing and Steno-graphy—Manuscripts—Public Accounting— that was how she advertised herself in the paper (a writer who couldn't type his own manuscripts was in any case a pain in the neck) and here Adam suddenly closed his eyes a moment trying to black out the pictures that flashed into his mind, for he did not see Patsy stiff and attentive, with her pencil poised for dictation, nor did he see her at a typewriter with her nimble fingers playing swiftly over the keys—no indeed—God no, he saw her lying on Philip Ropes's couch, beautiful and naked, and Philip Ropes beside her, beautiful and naked too—that camellia-white body, those delicately-molded thighs, that soft red pubic hair, and her mouth (the taste of Patsy's lips), the flowerlike opening mouth. God, that was what he'd paid her for. He was dead certain of it, though she'd sworn it was not the case. And how the devil could she expect him to play pimp to Philip Ropes? Lord, he'd starve before he'd cash that check. He could beat his way until he got the money from the government—only another week until the GI check came in. A man could beg. The successful beggars were always the young men who looked as though they'd had an education, whose clothes and shoes and general appearance suggested a decent background. The poor fellows, reduced to this. All they had to do was to hold out the hand an hour or more. He could work a district where nobody had ever seen his face—upper Broadway around the Seventies. That's what he would do. Everything would be scheduled, everything sacrificed for work.

Damned dangerous intersection. Were the red lights holding him up or telling him to go? Getting a cartload full of books across Seventh Avenue right here with the trucks and taxis bearing down on him was something of a feat. He might as well be the old junk man. It somehow got him down. Well, here he was. Where did he go from here? Down Morton to Hudson, or through Bedford into Cherry Lane? Again he hauled the pushcart up.

No more dalliance. He was resolved to show some guts. He'd work on schedule. The first few days would be damned hard. But just as soon as he had dumped this stuff in his new room he'd get right out and do his little stint—extend the hand. It wouldn't be difficult to pick up a few dollars every day. Think of the material he'd be getting for his new novel, the real raw down-and-out stuff.

Compare his experience with the knowledge Philip Ropes had got of life—here Adam spat. There was this urgency, this sense of being driven. All the novels, the other young men. All the photographs on the backs of the dust jackets. There were hundreds of first novels—all the handsome young men with the blurbs that blew them up as large as Tolstoy, as large as Dostoevsky. It was like a contagion, some sickness of strife and competition, this chucking about of names and reputations. Why, you could put your finger on the very pulse-beats of other people's triumphs, everything so public and conspicuous. Life came at you in every direction. It was the hungers, the hungers in the heart were suspect.

Here now was his chance to slip through Bedford with free access to Cherry Lane. There was something ganging up on him, weighing down his spirits—the anguish of the days ahead, getting into the rut. The whole terrific business of mastering his craft, breaking the backs of sentences, assailed him—just plain learning how to write. What relentless memories, sitting at his typewriter for hours sweating blood, his eyes gone bleary, tired in every bone and sinew, his nerves frazzled like so many snapping fiddle strings, not able to write a decent paragraph, running to the nearest bar to fortify himself with as much liquor as he could pay for, coming back and trying to wrench his style from other novelists. Why, he had at one time mastered all O'Hara's tricks and mannerisms; he'd copied Hemingway, he'd tried his hand at Sartre, but Joyce was and always would be the master who would drive him to despair. He knew what he was after, he had everything to say; he'd experienced plenty.

Philip Ropes, what did he know about anything, the little dilettante who couldn't even type his manuscript, getting Patsy in to dictate, walking up and down and dropping the immortal sentences? Such a handsome fellow with his chestnut curls and his collar open at the neck, a swell face for the dust jackets. Couldn't you just see that face embellishing the blurbs? Hallo, the Cherry Lane theater—presenting a play by Sartre. He drew up a moment to inspect the bill. Now there was a writer who knew just what he was about, went directly to the heart of the matter. He'd never have begun a novel with reveries and reminiscences, giving you back your streets and moods and memories—far too explicit for that. He would have started off with Patsy in that bed in Jones Street. He'd have described the bed, warm and consoling, and Patsy, beautiful and naked in the bed beside him on that memorable night when all their troubles had begun. He'd have guessed exactly how she felt about Philip Ropes, conjuring up that peerless young man, while she lay there letting him make love to her—vicarious pleasure, that's what he'd accused her of experiencing. Patsy had denied it. She'd said that she was sick and tired of him and his everlasting analysis, trying to fix up situations out of every moment, complicating everything; there was no freedom, no frankness left, no simplicity. Well, she was right, there hadn't been. Her every tremor now involved with Philip Ropes; you couldn't fool him about women.

Trundling through Cherry Lane into Barrow, down Barrow, crossing Hudson with the lights now in his favor his bitterness accumulated. That tone of voice in which she'd said "there's your precious manuscript," the amount of sarcasm which she'd managed to put into those few words persisted. It hadn't been too long ago that Patsy had believed he was her little genius.

What a fuss she'd made about him, persuading him to give up his perfectly good job and stick exclusively to writing. She'd forced him into it. It was a crime for anyone with such creative gifts to use up all his energies on work that he despised. Where was he now? Back with his GI checks and his little course in English. She loved her little geniuses. Well, he had done with women. They didn't jibe with work. The sooner he was down to good hardpan, the better—loneliness, misery, solitude. That was his receipt. He would with the greatest willingness make Patsy over to Philip Ropes. He could have her.

Down Barrow to Greenwich Street. He looked up at the houses. Patsy had told him they were so cute. Little red houses, dormer windows. Cute enough. Why shouldn't he cash that check? After all, whose fault was it that he was down and out? He'd paid the bills when first he'd gone to live with Patsy. He stopped and took the check out of his pocket. Made out to Patricia Smith, signed by Philip Ropes the third and countersigned by Patsy. Quite a story in it, a little story à la Chekhov called "The Check." Should he cash it, should he tear it into ten thousand bits? He returned it to his pocket. He turned the corner into Greenwich Street. The cute little houses continued; but what a difference! What a dismal street— all these trucks that rumbled past the windows and that big ugly building opposite, United States Post Office, mail trucks coming, mail trucks pulling out. Here he was, one of the little red houses all right but what a dingy look to it. Gardens behind, she'd said, and little dormer windows; cute as all get-out. But what good would they do him—living in the basement? Leaving the pushcart on the curb he climbed the stoop and let himself in with a key Patsy had procured from the janitor (he was presumably Patsy's brother)— good thing the rent was paid a week in advance.

God, what a stinking hole. He descended the basement stairs, opened and stumbled through a narrow hall to the front, opened and unlocked a sagging door, and found himself in a dark square room below the level of the street, with a very musty odor. It appeared to be furnished. There were two small windows with an outer iron grille giving on a hatchway. He threw them open. Jesus, what a hole. A closed-up fireplace with a black marble mantelpiece adorned one side of the room, and opposite a cot with a green plush spread and two green plush cushions propped against the wall. The floor was covered with a worn linoleum rug, there was a Morris chair by the window upholstered in plum-colored corduroy, very worn indeed, a wooden rocking-chair, and in the center of the room under a cluster of electric lights a rickety table with a marble top. He went to the bed, felt the mattress, sat down on it, smelled the sofa cushions. Jesus Christ.

His eyes roamed around; took in a passage between his room and one at the back which presumably opened into that garden that Patsy had boasted of, "all those dear little red brick houses opening on their gardens." He got up, went through the passage, tried the door which was locked and bolted. There were cupboards and running water—everything necessary as Patsy had said. He turned on the taps; the water ran. Well, he'd be damned. Now, what he'd have to do was pull himself together and get his junk in out of the rain.

It seemed like an interminable business, dumping first one load and then another, no order about it, helter-skelter, pell-mell, angrily making the trip to the sidewalk and back to his room Lord knows how many times. It was somnambulistic, like a dream he'd had before and expected to have innumerable times again, realizing too that he was just one in a regiment of GI brothers having their little love affair with art and the humanities. Here were these folders (the precious manuscript Patsy had been so sarcastic about). Under the bed with it, safe from the rest of the litter. Well, to what else could you turn your allegiance, if you didn't turn to art? Perambulating the room, taking up this book and that and his eyes roaming round, it seemed to him he was surrounded by masterpieces, cheap editions, the big Giants, and the smaller volumes. God, the room was filled with masterpieces—translations, anthologies—that banged-up box was stuffed with masterpieces, if you turned the right knob at the right moment, they flew into it from the very air you breathed. The records, the victrola, Picasso's *Clowns*. Did the fellows making up statistics in the government bureaus get wind of all this, so many GIS at this university, so many at that, all his brother veterans attempting to drink from every spring at once? For here was art, the aristocratic, the inaccessible commodity, suddenly made cheap, mass-produced like everything else. You had to hasten, there was a fearful and immoderate haste about it. With the whole of society geared up to the organized production of murder, wholesale slaughter, you had to choose your horse and mount in haste, art and death running it neck and crop.

Suddenly he seemed to hear again that incredible accumulating volume of sound, and to see the heavens literally sundered to let pass above his head the majestic procession, thousands of planes roaring like express trains through the sky. God, the perfect synchronization, the order and the majesty, morning after morning at the punctual hour, all those bombers on their way to murder old men, children, babies, women, to blow up munition factories. It wouldn't be so majestic the next great show they staged. Likely to be silent, out of sight, out of sound. Some solitary bomber silent in the stratosphere on its way, God knows where, carrying God knows what infernal freight. Well, stick to the horse you've chosen, hurry, hurry like the devil. The race was not entirely reputable either, there were the rivalries, the jealousies, the triumph so public and conspicuous and he saw, though it was the very last thing he wished to see, the picture of Philip Ropes decorating the dust covers, all the blurbs, all the handsome young men who had snatched right out of the jaws of death you might say their little moment of success, flying into the magic beam, gyrating crazily in the public neon.

God, life came at you from every direction—all the thirsts and hungers that beset you. There was this Babel of voices—literatures, philosophies, distractions—there was the music, wanting to hear it all. It was free now—loose on the air, incised on the rubber discs, canned for your convenience if you had the price for it. Hurry, hurry. And there were the pictures, the exhibitions, the museums, the art shops. No, it was not just the drive to create something on your own; it was these little empires of beauty you needed to build up in your solitary soul, call it culture if you wish to, universal culture, poets, scholars, anthropologists, historians, theologians, philosophers contradicting, asserting, and the musicologists, the art critics, the reviewers—such a babel of tongues, such exquisite distractions, clutching at them all. Good God, thinking you could read, hear, see, *get* everything all at once, these thirsts and hungers to be assuaged, wanting to drink from all the springs at once, snatching at universal culture, being, as you damned well knew you were, the most solitary, the most lonely individual that ever at any moment in the march of mad events had trod upon the earth.

It was multitude from which we suffered, all that everybody had to tell us, buzzed around and blown upon by all the conversations and the arguments. Our traffic with each other, what a queer attempt to protect our aloneness. Christ, how we loved our own aloneness. We did plenty of howling about it, it was a central theme of all our art expressions. None the less we hugged it jealously. We were incapable of giving because there was so much within our reach to grab and snatch and gather for our own, our solitary souls.

Take his relationship to women. Always the same old story. There was Patsy now—her fresh, her lovely body; yet the more he ravished it, the closer he drew to it, the farther she retreated with her loneliness, the more she cherished her little empire of selfhood, extending it, hoarding it up, subjecting each experience to analysis, to some damned way or another of getting wise about herself. It was just this of which she had complained to him about his own behavior. What was it she had said had made her sick of him, sick and tired of this way he had—taking the pulse of each vibration?

He flung himself down on the bed. He was mortal fagged. This putting the energies and muscles to work on tasks so uncongenial drained the life blood out of him. He'd never set this place to rights. God!—what a hole in the wall—the worst he'd ever had. He buried his face in the green plush cushions. Phooey, how they stank! Imagine sleeping on a bed like this. He groaned.

My Old Lady—Mol! Why not call her up and ask her to cash this check? Simple enough. Hadn't he been suppressing his resolve to do so right along? Sure he had. The money was his. It wasn't as though it came to him from Ropes. It was the payment of a debt. Patsy owed it to him. Why be so stiff-necked about it? Ridiculous to think he could beat it, beg his way until he got the GI check.

Mol—what a queer, eccentric bird she was. He had a real affection for her. When he came right down to it, he'd have to admit she was the only human being in this benighted city who really cared for him. Absurd she was, caring so much about the bloody world, so dramatic about everything, beating her chest and flashing those astonishing eyes. "If you'd lived as long as I have, my dear boy," always getting back at him with her age and her experience. She seemed to him, in spite of all the books she'd read and her fine assumption of knowing all there was to know, innocent as a May morning; virginal he'd swear.

The longer he lay here and tried to make up his mind to telephone, the less likely he'd be to find her in. It must have stopped raining by now. Very likely she'd be out. He got up, and going to the window, craned his neck to see just what the day was like.

Jesus, you couldn't see the sky. There above the area railing was the sidewalk and the pushcart, and both quite dry. He supposed he'd have to trundle the old cart back to the ice and wood man from whom he'd rented it.

Okay, the sooner he was out of this black hole, the better. He searched his pants to find the check, looked at it, put it in his waistcoat pocket, buttoned up his coat. Now to discover if he had some change. Why, he'd be damned. The Lord was on his side. Here was fifty cents, here was a nickel. He'd go out now and find the nearest drug store.

Mol—My Old Lady—he said, as he groped his way through the dark hall to find the outer door. She'd let him have the cash.

THREE

There had been of course, thought the old woman as she reflected on her childhood and the manuscript she was about to read, the two large inhospitable houses where she had been so lost and so unhappy, the Fosters and the Chamberlains and all the rest of them walking about among their splendid properties. But there had also been the outdoor, the open world—certain experiences looked forward to each year, annually repeated and becoming, as the seasons circled round her completing the cycle of the years and memories, the very essence of life and anticipation. Winter and spring, summer and the autumn: yes, that was their sequence in her memory.

Winter!—it was the cold smell, the no-smell, snow smell, the first flakes falling on the mittens, on the coat sleeves, and never one exactly like another, it was those storms that changed the rhythms of the blood and the behavior of the nerves, the wind blowing the white dust off the drifts, swathing the lawns, whirling the snow up in a great darkness, sucking it like a typhoon into the cloud, sweeping it from the roofs of houses, from the boughs of trees, creating such a dark the flying flakes were lost to sight. The lull, and snowfall seen again, that soft accumulation of the flakes.

It was the clear cold days that followed, the glitter of the sun upon the snow, the lambent shadows on the lawn, the fiery incandescent atoms dancing, gyrating by their billions and quadrillions in the air. It was the breath that streamed before her as she walked, the snow creaking beneath her shoes, the numbed face and feet and not a thing to smell but the sharp keen no-smell of the cold. The sudden thaws, the drip, drip, dripping from the eaves, the sound of icicles shattering as they fell, snowballs easy to manufacture, the mittens soaked, the coat hem drenched. It was scent returning to the breath, memory stirring, rain and again the cold and all those crystal exhibitions, groves and gardens, fountains, pavilions, palaces of ice—sights glittering and splendid but unrelated, severed from the flow. And finally, finally, communications, whispers, that little mesh and maze of sparrow voices and the whir of sparrows wings, the gutters running rivers and the grass exposed, feet sinking in the mud, rubbers sucked clean off the shoes, roots stirring—intimations, memories, buds swelling on the boughs of trees.

Spring was that swamp where all the violets grew in such abundance, variously tinted, poised and spurred, the large deep blues, those with large white faces delicately penciled, the short-stemmed red variety, and always when she saw them that sense of having been divinely conducted to some secret ground.

It was that search for flowers in the woods, the spell cast over her, the light dim, the stillness of a place enclosed. Above, the brown buds sheathed in their brown casings casting gloom upon the light that filtered through the boughs, and on the ground to the right and to the left all the adorable green shoots and tendrils, the little antic flowers of the woods springing to life and vigor among the skeletal leaves, the dry dead needles of the pine, ferns pushing their unfurled fronds above the earth, standing about like little wool-clad gnomes in the grotesquest attitudes, stems of the moss tipped with the minutest blossoms. And there on that bed of rusty, far from springlike leaves, arbutus, perfect and precise as stars, pink as though they had been washed in the pure waters of the dawn, peering up at her—kneeling to pick them, burying her face in the evanescent, the ineffable fragrance, that sense she'd had of waiting on some memory, some intimation, of having been—but when but where she could not tell.

Summer was that field on the high shelf above the ocean, the meadow-larks rising, the bobolinks swinging on the timothy. It was that dance of joy, that dance of life, that perfect union with the summer day, exact accord with all the little flying creatures and the business they accomplished, something physical about it, visceral, planted very deep in memory, singing with the larks, skimming with the swallows, everything barging up, blowing up, buzzing, humming, floating—all the white, the innocent daisies, the oxeyed daisies, the buttercups, and the grasshoppers transparent as the grass, hopping, springing, squatting, working their horses' jaws, making spittle on the grass blades, and some of them with wings shaped like little fans, opening and shutting them with such a clack and clatter, flying in every direction, the butterflies descending noiseless on this flower and on that, spreading the velvet and the satin, here the yellow, there the purple, the cat's eyes, the tiger's stripes. Running here, running there, and something in her crying out to that blue, mysterious element beyond the dunes to wait, to keep its distance, to allow her still a little longer to belong completely to the earth.

It was that swift descent upon the beach, the surf strong, the waves breaking. Something pretty terrible about it—getting it in one fell swoop, the fury of the breakers carried back to crash and echo in the dunes, waves running up the shore in all their sound and smother, the wild cold smell of the salt spray inducing maniac excitement. Up the path of the waves shrieking, down the hard wet slope again, the waves springing, leaping forward, and one more terrible than all the others standing up in its intolerable beauty, seeing the jellyfish and seaweed and the flung sand churned within its glassy caverns, hearing amid the roar and thunder that little dreadful music of the bubbles breaking, opening their lips on air, on sand, on stone.

Autumn was the orchard where she used to come to bury katydids and spiders, and a state of the clammiest contentment—the air webbed with all manner of tiny tunes and gossamer occurrences, gnats humming, flies and bees and hornets droning, shining threads attached to no visible bough or leaf or spider slack in the bright air, wings flashing, vanishing, bits of down and fluff and feather disappearing in the blue, appearing in the sunlight, those fat worms squirming loose from the grave she opened, and the sepulchral smell of the autumnal earth.

But not a word of all this recorded in that manuscript, she thought as she rose to take her novel from the desk where it had lain so long unread.

FOUR

Miss sylvester turned the pages of the manuscript, and moved at once into that dim abyss of time where recollections dawned, where rooms gave off their smells, their voices and associations. That sense she'd had of coming from nowhere into somewhere very large and most important back upon her in all its original assertiveness, she seemed to be groping rather blindly through her grandmother's home in Brookline.

How large the rooms had seemed—immense, falling away into echoing vistas, overfurnished, over-subdued by the weight of all those Victorian possessions. There was the wide hall, with doors opening on the double parlors, the library, the dining room, and at the end of the hall, and directly opposite the front door, that staircase, of splendid proportions, branching off with carpeted stairs and a balustrade on either side to meet a balcony halfway up and ascend again in all the majesty of its double flights to the floors above. Here more than elsewhere the large and lavish manner of the household had seemed to her exhibited. People ascended and descended. Some took the flight to the left, some the flight to the right. Maids in black dresses tricked out in clean white caps and aprons answered bells; they ran up and down in a flutter of apron strings and messages to be delivered; they came bearing boxes of flowers, candy boxes, boxes from the milliner's and huge important-looking boxes from the dressmaker's. Something about that stairway—the echoing rooms above and the echoing halls below that intimated the cramped, the meager, the not to say demeaning nowhere from which she had emerged into all this hustle and bustle, and how frequently she must have wondered, peering through the banisters, traveling up and down, what in the world she was doing amid all this important traffic.

Downstairs the large rooms, their lofty doors and ceilings, the high windows draped in heavy lambrequins and curtains, seemed to diminish her height and give her a curious sense of walking very lightly on her feet. All was reflection, scintillation—mirrors, chandeliers with pendant lusters, lamps, statuary, porcelain vases, marble busts, marble mantelpieces reduplicated down a vast extension of the scene.

There had been—most awe-inspiring of all the apparitions— old George the butler, carrying trays, announcing visitors. There were uncles, cousins, acquaintances engaged in animated conversation. Some sat down, some stood up, and anyone was likely at any moment to make a grab for her, to hold her at arm's length and exclaim, "Oh, *this* is the Sylvester child." The difference in the behavior of the sexes was very noticeable indeed. The ladies' laughter was light and musical, they affected the most decorative attitudes, their dresses fitted them closely, their waists were incredibly small, they wore the loveliest of hats. The gentlemen guffawed and gesticulated. They were extremely elegant. Some had beards carefully trimmed, some had mustaches meticulously combed, some wore clothes that gave them a curious robinlike appearance, some were dressed in coats which lent them a grave, ministerial look. The young men, with the notable exception of Lucien Grey, had clean faces and were more graceful and appealing than their elders. Young or old, male or female, they all had the unmistakable look of being very fashionable indeed.

Arriving with a heart from which all references had been erased, and bringing with her not a sight or sound or smell that might illuminate the past and thus explain the present, she'd had perforce to reconstruct it all as best she could. Vaguely realizing there was mystery behind her and a conspiracy of silence imposed upon a time when with a legitimate equipment of parents she must presumably have lived elsewhere, she had been accompanied by a curious sense, not only of trying to rediscover them, but in a measure of attempting, you might say, to find herself.

All was at first confusion, people holding her attention, flitting off again, an inflection of speech, an exaggeration of dress or gesture, the bird on Cousin Cecilia's hat, the way Great-Uncle William shrugged his shoulders, the scent that issued from a gown or handkerchief, a reprimand, some emphatic expression of opinion—figures, personalities, characters coming at her, retreating, coming at her again with an accentuation of their tricks of speech or gesture, their private queernesses and mannerisms, until, lo, behold, what with piecing all the impressions together, responding to them with the uncanny sharpness that her position of insecurity somehow or other induced, she became acquainted with her grandmother and grandfather, the formidable great-aunts and uncles, her beautiful Aunt Eleanor, and Lucien Grey, with Cousin Cecilia Ware, and her pretty, frivolous Aunt Georgie. She observed them with a kind of spellbound attention and was never without a feeling that they were actors taking part in a series of improvised scenes and exhibitions, fascinating but not altogether enjoyable. Something seemed to be lacking, some warmth, some sense of being attached to people and things, and not just suffered to walk around among them.

Difficult to tell what exactly happened when in that crowded world to which she had become attached, rooms, conversations, people and the manners they carried about with them, shifting and changing as they did in memory, but there was a certain emotional climate which persisted throughout those first winters in Brookline, induced by plans, postponements, preparations—bringing Aunt Georgie out into society, getting her successfully married. The entire house vibrated to these events, and as it comes back to her, all this stir of talk and preparation seemed to have sharpened and increased a feeling she carried uneasily about of being somehow or other responsible for holding up the schedule of events, arriving as she had in a shroud of mourning that suspended all festivities and left all projects hanging in the air. It must have been the "coming out" which her arrival had actually delayed. But nonetheless, the great occasions became inextricably combined in mood and in memory, and as far as her responses to them went, they seem now to have taken place but once, and to have brewed in her heart exactly similar impressions. And how she had been able, amid those glittering displays of family pride and power, to make out that she in her small person represented something that had run amok in worldly calculations it is impossible to explain. Wandering about amid those tides of merriment, congratulations, laughter, and with the strains of flute and fiddle, the fragrance of innumerable hothouse flowers, the subtlest perfumes wafted to her from the circulating ladies, heightening her emotions and inscribing on her sensibilities God knows what of melancholy pleasure, she had been most certainly aware that she stood somehow for misfortune, not to say disgrace.

That daughters must marry into their own class and maintain their position in society was an essential doctrine held by both her grandparents. For what earthly reason had they elected to marry and bring them into the world if not for such alliances? The roots and reasons for these assumptions she was, naturally enough, unable to plumb, but somehow or other she had been able to pluck from the very air around her, through hints and inflections, through words and phrases far from clearly understood, the realization that her mother had brought disgrace upon the Fosters and the Chamberlains, and though she was completely ignorant of the story attaching to her parents, she seemed to have suspected very early in the game that her mother had never been properly "brought out" nor decently married.

Some talk overheard among the servants about a runaway match should have set her right on the details, but knowing nothing about matches except that she was forbidden to strike them because of fire, and runaways in this connection suggesting fire engines—horses running to a fire, the phrase served only to confuse. All this was presently cleared up, but for a while she knew only that her mother had died and "gone to heaven," as good old Irish Annie frequently assured her, "to live with God," and as she heard nothing at all about the other parent she simply had taken it for granted that he was also dead and residing happily in heaven.

An inclination on everybody's part to act as though she had come parentless into the world could not, very naturally, persuade her that this was the case and there was that house that had for some time had the power, whenever she so much as thought about it, to scare her out of her wits, a symbol of her dreadful, her demeaning past. This nightmare sense of it came to her full-fledged out of that incident that had occurred on a spring morning in the nursery when certain shabby trunks and boxes from "the house in Pinckney Street" were brought down from the attic to be unpacked. Grandmother Foster supervised the whole performance and there had been something about her expression, the way she handled, smelled and sorted out the various articles—blankets, sheets and little undergarments, dresses, coats and jackets, undoubtedly her own—that had suggested as she watched her from the floor where she remembers she was seated the very direst kind of poverty; and when she heard her add, "These will be quite suitable for Joe, I understand his daughter has a brood of little girls," the final touch of the macabre and dreadful was put upon her speculations. For was not Joe, the old man who came out from Boston to assist the gardener (Dago Joe as Annie called him), an Italian as well as a Dago and had she not somewhere ascertained the fact that her own father was an Italian and learned moreover that he was a musician, and was it not most logical to jump to the conclusion, having in this musical connection only a hand organ to rely upon, that he was a Dago organ-grinder? Anyway it was thus she'd made it out, leaping wildly from one association to the next, as she sat there on the floor and watched her grandmother handling, sorting, *smelling* those little garments, and heard her in that high and lofty way she had bestowing them upon that scary old man, and from that day on and for some time afterwards poverty, parents, Pinckney Street were trammeled up together, to breed in her imagination a series of the most sordid and frightening pictures—men and women with tattered sleeves and toes protruding from their shoes and wearing the most disreputable of hats, lurking in area-ways, poking in the ashcans, children with uncombed hair and uncouth manners playing in the gutters and in the vicinity of garbage cans, and naturally enough, the Dago organ-grinder with his organ and his monkey and his cup extended grinding out his scary tunes.

Just how long this ghoulish sense of her forgotten past prevailed she cannot be quite sure, but she remembers perfectly the day that it was dissipated and the delight and surprise that she experienced and how then and there her mind escaping the dark and horrid speculations seemed to run at once toward new and happier conclusions and how she was immediately furnished with a succession of the most romantic, comforting, and comfortable beliefs.

Oh, the vividest memory of that experience comes back—the cold crisp weather, the sharp astonishment, the unutterable relief, driving on one of those rare occasions when she went to town with her grandmother in an open sleigh, that delicious sense she had of almost sliding along on air, all so smooth and swift and sunny. Her grandmother beside her silent in her sealskin coat, then suddenly leaning forward and saying to the coachman in her peremptory way—"Turn here into Pinckney Street—stop at twenty-eight."

Pinckney Street! To say that she was filled with horror, with a kind of dreadful expectation is to put it mildly. The sleigh turned. My goodness gracious! How astounding—bewildering indeed! It was a very pleasant kind of street, not perhaps as elegant as other streets she'd seen, but none the less tidy, clean. They stopped at twenty-eight. Could this be perhaps the house, the awful house of her imaginings? There were curtains in the windows, the stoop was well swept. The footman jumped down, climbed the steps, rang the bell. What a pleasant house! What a pleasant street, clean, tidy—people on the sidewalks were dressed in the most respectable clothes, no uncouth children played in the gutters, there were no terrifying women in tattered clothes with unkempt hair picking over garbage cans; not a drunken man in sight.

The door was opened, a maid appeared and took the letter. The footman descended the steps, clambered to the box. The horses neighed and shook their bells and pranced away.

What relief, what joy! Her parents had not lived in a place of horror, in a dreadful slum. Her father was not, he had never been a Dago—no Dago could have lived in such a street! And then and there her mind went skipping in and out of words, incidents, references she didn't even realize she'd remembered; and with a speed, a brilliance that was nothing short of unbelievable, piecing this and that and utterly discarding all that had been distressing and confusing, the runaway horses and the fire engine as well as the monkey and the organ-grinder retreating forever into limbo, her parents' gallant little love affair came to her as clear as day and infinitely brave and true. Of course that runaway match meant simply this, that her mother had run away with the Italian musician, who had married her and brought her to Pinckney Street to live. Just to think of her having had the courage to do such a thing—defying and standing out against Grandmother Foster, who, as far as she'd been able to discover, nobody dared so much as contradict. Gracious, how she must have loved him! Why, he had not been an organ-grinder at all. Far from that! Suddenly, in a flash of what must have been sheer clairvoyance, she'd got it all exactly right, brushed as she had been in that miraculous instant by the memory of what Grandfather Foster had said when he'd come upon her in the parlor at The Towers sitting on the musical chair, "The Overture to *William Tell,* your father's favorite tune," receiving instantly (the silvery tune the chair gave off perhaps assisting in this feat of memory and intuition) the picture of a dark Italian elegantly attired standing up before her straight and slender, playing on a flute.

Doubtless the fact that he had played in the Symphony Orchestra got hitched to all these intuitions at a later time, so curiously do recollections lapse and come together in the mind, but in retrospect it seems to her she'd got the whole thing in that bright moment straight. The sleigh continued to slip merrily along, and oh how proudly she surveyed Pinckney Street, how she regretted that she was not living there as she must have done before she remembered anything about it. However, she could bear to be without her parents if she could cherish in the thought of them such a romantic story—keep them forever beautiful and brave—mysteriously touched by death.

FIVE

The years did not diminish her treasure, which due to the consolations of good Irish Annie added the joy of anticipation to the satisfaction she somehow felt in the possession of parents who had, according to Annie, so beautifully "gone before." The idea of joining them in heaven began to dawn, and presently took on all that could be imagined of the gala and familiar as well as the supernatural and divine. Heaven became for her a very actual place, and she found no difficulty at all in combining the joys of earthly greetings on the part of those long separated and bereaved with states of more seraphic and transcendent bliss. It seemed simple enough to imagine an ambient where they were invested with the human as well as the angelic condition. Since it existed both in her mind and heart and memory, she required for its architecture no more than what her eyes had looked upon with wonder and delight—the morning and the evening clouds together with all the bright stars strewn upon the sky and all the lovely flowers growing in the grass. It was a place immense and capable of infinite extension, with clouds perpetually opening to reveal unending corridors—vistas of mountains, valleys, rivers, seas. So vast indeed as to allow all the dead and all the living, those who had died before and those who at some time in the future would be dead, to meet and recognize each other and to renew their earthly ties at just that instant when clothed in their flesh and bones they had been so rudely torn apart and where among all these human and bodily reunions divine and incorporeal changes were perpetually taking place—children turning into angels, parents flying about on angelic wings and God Himself at the center of all the light and splendor forever welcoming the newcomers—bidding them draw a little nearer to His throne.

Yes, that was about as she had pictured it—dying and going to heaven—and though she was by no means frequently visited by these divine anticipations nonetheless they vaguely fringed her reveries whenever she dwelt at any length on the thought of her parents, both of whom, for she had heard nothing to the contrary, had died and gone, as Annie used to tell her, to heaven to live with God.

And it was certainly because of these bright mansions of her imagination that Easter became the day of all days in the year to be anticipated. How vividly she gets those Easters back, the beauty of the season and her delight in being dressed as gaily as the spring. That drive to Boston accompanied by her grandparents, and oh, so happily aware of the new shoes and coat, the straw hat trimmed with its bright wreath of Easter flowers, the special sense she'd had of it, spring and joy and resurrection, gaining momentum as they drove along, the church bells on the air, the children on the sidewalks carrying pots of flowers contributing enormously to her peculiar joy. Why, by the time she arrived at church and alighted from the carriage, it had reached a peak of the highest solemnity. Walking down the aisle behind the grandparents, she was, you might say, drenched, baptized in Easter sentiment. What with the profusion of spring flowers massed beneath the windows and banked upon the altar, and that cool sweet smell of Easter lilies flowing through the other perfumes like the very breath and fragrance of the day, the glory spread, became a great effulgence streaming from her heart. The organ voluntary rolling through the aisles and arches seemed to be rolling back the clouds of heaven. They bloomed, they burst asunder. Aware that her acquaintance with loss had left her open to receive the glory and the splendor, she was translated, lifted in her new spring coat and hat right into heaven.

On this memorable Sunday Easter was as she recounts it unusually late, and the drive home after church delightful with the trees in leaf and the birds caroling away. But what stood out so clearly in her mind was her grandfather's high spirits and that after-church solemnity that enveloped her grandmother, and how suddenly out of a portentous silence she remarked, "Let the dead past bury its dead. Do not speak of it again. Treat the event as though it had not occurred." To all of which her grandfather, continuing his whistling, folded his arms without rejoinder.

This had left within her heart an area of apprehension, some sense that it could not go without a sequel, an expectation carried with her to the dinner table, and she cannot now go over the dramatic disclosures that finally ensued without feeling she is there in that familiar room, seeing the picture, vivid, animated, before her eyes—the table drawn out with all the extra leaves set in to its extremest length, the damask cloth of incredible dimensions, the napkins folded to look like Easter lilies, displaying their embroidered monograms, and all the plates, the knives and forks and spoons, the goblets and wineglasses set to such absolute perfection, the flowers in the center of the table so fresh, with the ferns, the daffodils and freesia and narcissus doing their best to conceal the painted eggs so discreetly hidden in their midst, all the festival decorations, the gold-and-lace-fringed snappers, the place cards, the bonbon containers adding a touch of the naive and childish to this positively regal laying out of the best family glass and napery and china.

There they all were, the various members of her extraordinary family, Aunt Georgie, Charlie Lamb, Aunt Eleanor and Lucien Grey, Cousin Cecilia Ware, the great-uncles and their wives, Uncle William and Aunt Mary, Uncle Richard, Aunt Amelia, Uncle James, Aunt Harriette, and she in their midst, with Lucien on one side of her and Great-Uncle William on the other, perfectly certain that something was about to occur.

Dinner went on as usual. The familiar jokes and platitudes from everybody, the change of plates, and finally the arrival of the champagne, Grandfather accomplishing his part of all this business with his usual grace, extracting the first cork and then out of the smoking bottle, without so much as spilling a single drop, pouring a little of the sparkling wine into his glass. With equal grace he opened a second bottle and a third.

The wine went round the table. Everyone's glass was filled. The Easter toast, "To the family, the living, and the dead," was downed. Then Grandfather got up. "Let us drink," he said, "to the burial of the feud."

And then all the voices, all the questions, everything so quick, so surprising—getting the startling news trying to adjust to it, sitting there stunned, bewildered. "Horace!" her grandmother's voice so sharp and so peremptory, and Aunt Eleanor, "What feud, Papa?" and all together taking up her grandfather's announcement.

"Silvestro's dead. He's had the grace to take himself off."

"You mean to say," Uncle William sputtered it out, "Silvestro's dead?" And Uncle Richard, "I was under the impression that he was long since dead—or as good as dead." And Uncle James, "Suicide, eh? the poor fellow did away with himself?"—"James!" Aunt Harriette, she remembers, casting an eye in her direction.

"He couldn't have done *that*, Papa," from Aunt Eleanor.

And here it was that Lucien Grey had laid his hand on hers, the two of them caught up together, listening.

"Oh," Grandfather said, "we needn't call it that. The poor fellow fell off a cliff. You know they have 'em in the south of Italy—lots of cliffs and vineyards on the top of 'em."

"Horace," from her grandmother, reprimanding him down the length of that long table.

"Lucky thing!" muttered Uncle William, still gobbling his lamb. "No more trouble from that direction."

"Well, I can't say," her grandfather corrected, "that we did have any trouble from him, since he took himself away to Italy—signed the papers and all."

"Horace!" Grandmother's voice had risen to a shriek.

"But you never can tell," he said, "it's a good thing for everyone concerned the poor fellow's out of it."

How could she possibly have digested it? The ice cream, she remembers, was presently brought on, a great pink and white and chocolate colored lamb, with flowers for ears and spun sugar all around the platter, and everybody, happy enough to change the subject, exclaiming how beautiful it was, and Grandfather giving her one of his famous winks, remarking that they'd slain the paschal lamb especially for her. Sitting there stunned and wondering who she was, Sylvester or Silvestro, and what she could make of a father who had not all these years been waiting in a condition of angelic expectation for her in heaven. He had been right here on earth, and made no attempt to get in touch with her—just taken himself off to Italy.

Now he was dead. There was something unforgettable about it all, trying to accommodate herself to the information, and with Lucien caught up in it, knowing the way she felt—sitting there and watching the ice cream go round the table, his hand on hers.

SIX

She closed her eyes and gave herself up to meditation. It was a curious thing, she thought, but she could not for the life of her remember—really remember Lucien. There were of course the amber eyes, the dark mustache, the mobile, enigmatic countenance, but when she tried to reconstruct his features, the expressions of his face, she could not make an image clear enough to bring him back as she had known him then.

For her now he represented all that overwhelming passion, that ecstasy and anguish, the sorrow and the severance which was to say the lamentable story of her love for him, and there were in this connection so many things still left to be conjectured, the fact that he belonged to that closed world, the world of Chamberlains and Fosters, of people walking about among their splendid properties, was naturally to be taken into account.

"Ah well." She looked out at the familiar buildings. The lights were extinguished except for a few scattered windows still bright in the Metropolitan Tower. "Ah well," she said, and there appeared upon her face an expression of profound gravity. Life was tragic enough in all conscience, but it had its exquisite comedy, and it was on this threshold, delicately poised between a comic and a tragic sense of it, she had first become aware of her friendship for Lucien Grey.

The chance and change of circumstance! Would her own personal tragedy have gathered to such a climax if she had not been seated next to Lucien on that particular Easter Sunday? Well, she concluded, very likely yes, what with those long summers he always spent at The Towers, each of them addicted as they were to scrutiny and observation, and their being thrown together among that gallery of characters. It was not only his sympathy but his sensing what a show it was, that exhibition of family obtuseness, that had made her feel for him such an ecstasy of gratitude—appreciation.

This exalted young man whom even Grandmother Foster held in such high esteem that she found it necessary whenever she spoke of him to say his name twice over, had all at once become a close companion, the two of them by some magic distillation of their qualities capable of passing signals, exchanging messages. How he had assisted her in her enjoyment of the human comedy, confirming her in a knowledge of something she had somehow from the very start seemed so intuitively to know—that there were no frontiers at all between the realm of laughter and the realm of tears. It was only necessary to meet his gaze, set up an interchange, a conversation which the very lack of speech converted into code, tossing the amusement back and forth between them, lifting the shoulders, and sometimes during those interminable midday dinners flicking little crumbs of bread across the table, and wanting desperately as she had on many an occasion to overturn the tumblers, to smash the china, to upset the general pomp and ceremony with a series of loud guffaws, saying as they often did between them, "Oh, really now, you do not mean to say so. We've heard all this a hundred times before." And watching Grandfather Foster as they might have watched a little monkey on a string, wishing that he would go to any length in his absurdities so they could appreciate the show the more, and always conscious of her grandmother, not unaware that there was something here more than a little frightening, as though she might at any instant come down upon their irreverence with some appalling reprimand, for she always seemed, with all her money and set round with these fine exhibits and displays, to have God upon her side; a presence to be feared, never letting anything escape her, and mistrusting the new relationship—her entering into cahoots with Lucien Grey.

To think of Lucien was always to think of those summers at The Towers. How clearly that incredible house of her grandfather's comes back to her. Shingled and clapboarded, perched up behind the hills and hollows of the dunes, with lawns in front of it and the blue ocean stretching off to meet the paler blue of the horizon, it stood, an architectural cross between the Kremlin and a cuckoo clock, adorned with towers and turrets, verandas, balconies, pavilions, the whole monstrous and elaborate structure painted various shades of green and yellow.

The rooms so full of voices, people long since dead, crossing the thresholds, leaving upon her as they passed the impact of their characters and eccentricities. Pretty rooms they were, frivolous and elegant, and filled with a prevailing pinkness, blueness, as of roses, hydrangeas, cupids generously distributed—flowery chintzes, Dresden ornaments, fresh-cut flowers, baskets upheld by cupids, little love seats, whatnots, shepherds, shepherdesses so gaily juxtaposed, and always the pleasant smell of sea and sand and honeysuckle freshly blown about.

The days were filled with people, arriving, departing. Festivities repeated themselves year after year to form one pattern in the memory; what with the garden parties, the tennis parties, her grandmother's afternoons at home, they seemed to merge into a single shifting panorama, the color and the movement all creating in her the same interior vibration and response. How vividly she visualized, how sharply she responded to it all again, those incredible green lawns, the flower beds, planted with ageratum, geranium and portulaca in the shape of anchors, hearts and half moons, set neatly in the grass, cannas waving from the borders and pink petunias fluttering above veranda rails, ladies carrying colored parasols, dressed in flowered hats and ruffled dresses, strolling about engaged in conversation, dappled with sun and shade, and gentlemen whose white ducks and flannels shone as bright as bright, passing refreshments, assisting in the general elegance. The movement, the voices, the cries and laughter, the ships and clouds and whitecaps, and the ocean breezes intermingling, wandering about in the deep recesses of her heart, accentuating that sense she carried with her of summer and the sea and heightening her excitement at the knowledge that among these alien people there was one voice, one face, one presence.

The only variation in the inward drama as the years progressed had been that increasing certainty she had that Lucien had made himself the guardian of her sensibilities. Being one of them himself, belonging to their world, how curious it was that he had been able to share her appreciation of those personalities, to watch them with her as though the two of them were nefarious spectators at a fascinating and continuous drama, the grandparents sharing the honors of the principals in the incredible performance.

What an astonishing pair they were! To think of them was to see them large as life and perfectly satisfied with themselves. How their presences assailed her even now. Her grandfather's elegance was simply beyond description. Even his mourning could not diminish it. When she encountered him first he affected, she remembered, broad black cravats adorned to strike the official note of grief with a large black pearl. He was small and dapper, and all this smartness and perfection assisted by the fragrance of eau de cologne and expensive soaps and pomades gave him a little breeze of his own which he wafted before him as he hurried here and there. His white hair sprang back from his head, framing to their very best advantage those fine features, that perfectly exquisite white mustache and the large dark eyes, the eyebrows impressively black were startling indeed—theatrical. Despite his mourning he was tuned to the enjoyment of life. What a lot of antic tricks and jokes he had, sticking his fingers in his ears and wagging them in a most alarming manner, and how he used to boo at her from behind closed doors and portieres. She had never been able to tell whether his exuberance or her grandmother's severity had been the more difficult to endure. The ordeal of sitting beside her grandmother in church was something to remember. Those Sunday clothes, that clean starched smell she had, the immaculate summer dresses without a spot or crease or stain, her little hats trimmed with such restraint and yet looking as though they'd cost a great deal of money, and the white gloves, so tight on the stout hands. There she'd sit, her hands folded in her lap, communing with God, never moving until some change in the service necessitated her standing up or falling upon her knees. Very pious she was, believing so implicitly that God was with her in all she did and said, and that towards the rich and the wellborn He extended His particular benevolence. How long she remained upon her knees, and when she'd got to her feet again, there was that look upon her marble countenance as though she were now doubly fortified in her belief in God and her own opinions.

Then there was Cousin Cecilia Ware, the ubiquitous poor relative, always managing to say the right thing at just the proper moment, "Yes, Cousin Amelia; yes, Cousin Horace"—making herself useful and somehow or other managing to keep herself so young and fresh and fashionable. Her outings with Grandfather Foster were, the weather allowing, a regular feature of those summer afternoons. She could see them starting off together as clearly as though the lively tableau were going on before her eyes.

Under the brightly painted porte cochere, the high, the brightly painted phaeton, the impatient horses, the small footman holding them in check. Then suddenly her grandfather making his appearance in spotless white, a flower in his buttonhole, his hat cocked a bit to one side, mounting to the driver's seat, putting on his gloves, taking up the reins, while Cecilia Ware clambered up to sit beside him, seated herself, opened her parasol, and the little footman, with the agility of an acrobat, jumped into the rumble as the horses reared and bolted off, adjusted himself to his precarious perch, crossed his arms upon his breast.

There on the sunny veranda stood her grandmother, her hand raised against the light, watching the animated spectacle. Laced and hooked and buttoned into her well-fitting costume as tightly as her emotions were packed into her breast, her face in some queer way resembled her figure. No betraying emotions save that look she had of paying strict attention to every detail. She noted with satisfaction that the footman's breeches were well chalked, his boots well shined, that the horses were in prime condition.

She approved the cut of Grandfather's coat, his way of handling the reins, she approved even of Cecilia, who bore herself in a manner that befitted her position.

She was well aware of the sentiments they entertained for each other, but she did not allow this to disturb her. Cecilia assisted her with her lists and made herself useful in many necessary ways; besides, she knew on which side of the loaf her bread was buttered. As for her little husband, if he wished to have an affair of the heart, much better to have it carried on right here beneath her eyes than in regions farther afield. She knew him to a T. He would never cross a single line she chalked for him. Moreover, he was always a perfect gentleman, an ornament to society. She regarded him, by and large, as the most elegant of all her appointments and accessories.

How Cecilia loved those drives, sitting there beside her dashing relative, fully conscious of the splendid appearance they presented to the world. It was not only the public show. She enjoyed his confidences, saying "Poor dear Cousin Horace," and making all those pretty sounds of condolence and acquiescence. She thought he was a creature of the deepest feeling, and as he had just such a notion of himself, his sensibility, his great capacity for suffering, no wonder they were never at a loss for sentimental conversation.

For years they had carried on a little affair of the heart. Fanned by all the breezes of mutual attraction, never allowed to go too far, each preserved unimpaired a sense of the other's charms. The glances they exchanged, the delicate breezes of sensuality they set afloat, did not, as she reflects upon it, escape her, and the fact that Grandfather Foster was as they used to put it "sweet upon Cecilia" created just another of those situations that she and Lucien shared together, and constituted some portion of that curious sense she had that matters of a nature somewhat secret and suppressed were under observation. Sex, if indeed she could speak of it as belonging to an age entirely unacquainted with the word, was for her a matter of the licensed exhibition, the small scenes and tableaux enjoyed with Lucien, all of which—the ladies in their low-necked dresses at the dinner table, their behavior at the garden parties, Charlie Lamb's lady-killing manners, Aunt Georgie's undisguised jealousy—savored more of the absurd and the ridiculous than of the passionate and profound.

Very dark and secret they had kept it. She had been led to understand that there were certain subjects under no circumstances to be mentioned. "When the proper time arrived," all would doubtless be revealed. She had been singularly lacking in curiosity. Her mind had been bereft of concrete facts, concrete sexual images. Perhaps it was the gallant little story of Silvestro and her mother where romantic love had captured her imagination as something belonging to the higher reaches of the soul, connecting it somehow with sorrow and her orphaned state, with evening and the falling of the dew, the scent of flowers in the garden. How oddly in her adolescence she had been assailed by longing, rushing off at twilight into the garden, or more often to the solitary beach, where she would throw her arms out wildly, invoking winds and waves: "Swiftly walk over the western wave, Spirit of Night"—what extraordinary power that particular poem had had, to fill her full of yearning, immense, unutterable, vague—"Out of the misty eastern cave / Where all the long and lone daylight / Thou wovest dreams of joy and fear / Which make thee terrible arid dear / Swift be thy flight!" And those ardent invocations at the end of every stanza, "Come soon, soon." For what was it she had waited? For love, for the arrival of a lover to whom she would yield up all the rich, the undiscovered treasures of her soul? Love had seemed to her as riotously, romantically incorporeal as those kisses of Shelley that mixed and merged with winds and waves and sunsets, leaving the soul quite free for unimpeded flights of poetry.

It had seemed to her quite possible that if two people actually in love with each other should, by some rare circumstance, be left long enough unchaperoned, their love might reach a climax of such soulful unity that the exchanging of a kiss, the extending of this rapture beyond the limits of propriety, might very possibly result in the shameful, the unlawful bearing of a child. It was thus she remembers she had interpreted that child, that scarlet letter pinned to the breast of Hester Prynne. And it was probably, she had made it out, to save her from just such ignominy that she was always so rigorously chaperoned, never allowed to be in the presence of a young man without Cecilia or Aunt Eleanor or someone of a proper age to see that the proprieties were kept.

How could she have been prepared for it, loving Lucien with her innocent, exclusive heart—that August afternoon when they had lain beside each other on the sand, the joining of their hands, their lips—the sudden tracks of fire traced along the secret pathways of her nerves, the secret channels of her blood?

How could she possibly have stood out against it, that sudden passionate love that consumed and overwhelmed her— those stealthy meetings under the lee of the dunes where very occasionally they used to lie together in the hot dry sand?

There were those words he used to whisper to her, "You are part of all things great and quiet, my beloved." She had thought them very beautiful. They were, he told her, taken from a Rumanian folk song. She had, to be sure, been very far from quiet. Her heart had beaten wildly when he took her in his arms. But after their love had been consummated, when all that passion was spent, there she'd lie, very quiet and meditative, listening while the waves approached and, breaking, drew back the pebbles with that mesmeric music that carried her away, floated her off across the waters, across the limitless horizons. Then it had seemed to her indeed she had become a part of that open world of childhood—those moments that were timeless and imperishable.

SEVEN

Very much absorbed she read on. Good gracious, she thought, her predicament had been incredible. Who would be able to believe in it? She found it difficult to believe in it herself and her mind running back to dwell on certain incidents that had preceded that memorable trip from Rome to Florence and which had so absorbed her thoughts upon that April day, she went over them again with all the old astonishment.

That morning at The Towers when Lucien and Eleanor had appeared so late for breakfast and something it had seemed to her between them—Eleanor with that look, hard to define it, in complete possession of her face and looking, if such a thing were possible, more beautiful than ever. Lucien pale, determined; he'd not looked up—he'd not looked at anyone and no sooner had he spread his napkin over his knees than he announced casually that he and Eleanor were leaving for the mountains—Eleanor he said had been suffering from lassitude. She needed a change of air. Eleanor kept her silence, that look of which she'd been aware spreading on her face and she remembers how she'd searched the other faces—Grandfather's evident surprise, blustering out his protest, "What, leaving for the mountains, wasn't the air here good enough for anyone?" and her grandmother sitting behind the coffee urn without a quiver of expression on her face—Lucien had done most of the explaining—a little as though he'd been talking to himself—for he'd looked at no one and it was sea level they'd seemed to be discussing—Eleanor had had too much of that—she needed higher altitudes and as the protests and expostulations had come entirely from her grandfather it was to be assumed that Grandmother Foster was in agreement—Eleanor must have a change.

At any rate, they had departed for the White Mountains that very afternoon. She'd had no word from Lucien. She had not laid eyes on him again until Thanksgiving when, politely, decorously, they had met in the big house in Brookline. At Christmas she had seen him, and during the winter they had met occasionally in the same casual family way, and he had discussed with her and the rest of them the plans her grandmother had made for her to spend accompanied by Cecilia a year in Europe just exactly as though nothing out of the ordinary had occurred. She would love Europe. He hoped she'd go to Italy. Not a word from anyone regarding her condition, merely that relentless carrying out of plans for Europe, and then, in February, his coming with all the others to see her off.

And oh, that moment on the steamer when they had been left alone together on the deck standing beside the rail. "Child," he'd said, his voice so broken he could not go on; the beating of her heart so loud she dared not look at him; and then Aunt Eleanor's arriving in a flurry of excitement, "Lucien, *who* do you think is on the boat—the Milton Steeles." She'd borne him off with her and that was the last she'd seen of him save for his face upon the pier among the other faces in the crowd.

Utterly incredible—never having mentioned her plight to a soul on earth and Cecilia playing her part to such perfection. Why no sooner had she been safely planted on foreign soil than she'd taken on the status of a respectable young matron—always referred to while they stayed in France as Madame and in Italy respectfully addressed as Signora. Goodness how Cecilia had loved it all—she'd positively doted on the coy little references—going in Paris to the dressmaker's to order the new spring clothes. Did Madame hope for *un fils* or *une fille*? and making the rejoinder as it were by proxy, "Oh, *un fils,* of course." And then in Rome how she'd enjoyed that too, being so conspicuous in her care of her—toting her about to see the sights and making such a feature of the fact that she was, impossible to disguise it, about to have a child.

So there, thought the old woman, continuing to read and to remember she'd been on that lovely day in April traveling from Rome to Florence and Cecilia beside her very smart in her Parisian outfit, the new spring suit and the fashionable hat that set off her little head and the blonde, the pretty puffs and curls so admirably, her manner arrogant and frivolous, playing the woman of the world. She was no longer the poor relation. She was acting the great lady for all she was worth—the garrulous, the asinine conversation, "Look, darling, the Maremma oxen, the beautiful Maremma oxen. Your grandfather loved the oxen. No wonder, with his beauty-loving soul."

There, opposite, was that sprucely turned-out little gentleman, who was, and it could not have escaped Cecilia's notice, an Italian version of Grandfather Foster, every move she made and every word she spoke a patent bid for his attention. "So good of your dear grandparents to send you to Italy at just this impressionable age. I wish I were seeing Italy for the first time." The old gentleman had crossed his knees and discreetly extended his well-shod foot in the direction of her pretty ankles.

Sooner or later, she had thought, they'd pick up an acquaintance. She'd given them however but scant attention, going back and forth among her memories, asking herself the same old questions, never able to answer them. Who had known exactly what, and above all, had Lucien been informed of her condition? She would wonder, what with his cousinages and connections, knowing he shared the same collateral relatives with Grandmother Foster, and remembering how she repeated his name twice over when she introduced him, "My son-in-law, Mr. Lucien Grey; Mr. Lucien Grey"—had not her grandmother let him off the final information? Could it be possible that Lucien had not known about the child? That was the all-important question.

On and on Cecilia prattled, "Look, darling, at that old monastery, see the priest under the cypresses reading his breviary. See the splendid villa, the stone pines along the avenue. Isn't Italy adorable?" And so on, and so on, until finally she'd leaned forward and tried, with a solicitude manufactured entirely for the benefit of the gentleman opposite, to place that little traveling pillow behind her back.

Was he or was he not informed? It was a question nobody was likely to ask or answer, so decorously and discreetly was everything proceeding. Round and round in a circle went her thoughts. What was going to happen next? The only thing she knew for certain was that Florence was her destination, and that Cecilia was carrying out her orders from behind the scenes, her grandmother's skillful hand directing every move. How supine she'd been about it all, never able to trump up the courage to have a showdown with Cecilia. What scenes and conversations she'd invented as she sat there, "See here, Cousin Cecilia, it's my right to know what you're planning to do with me and with my child," or, "Let's put an end to all this secrecy and make-believe"—forcing the issue in imagination as she sat beside her listening to the silly prattle.

She'd managed, as she knew she would, to get into conversation with her fellow traveler, and was doing her level best to draw her into it. "This gentleman has been so kind. He's been telling me about the places we must see while we're in Florence," and she'd turned to ask the name of that interesting little village he had spoken of.

"Borgo alla Collina." It meant, she'd explained, little town among the hills, and wasn't that perfectly charming? A very famous man was buried there. He was mentioned in Dante. They must not fail to go.

"The Signora is," she'd explained, "very interested in poetry. She intends to study Dante when she's mastered her Italian."

"Bravo," said the old gentleman.

She'd made no rejoinder whatever. She'd simply sat there, looking through the window at the broad, the spacious plain, the mountains, those celestial clouds and snows that lay upon them, and suddenly she'd felt consoled, carried beyond, outside her grief and her bewilderment. This is Italy, she'd thought, rejoicing in her Italian parent and in the radiant beauty of the Italian spring, all those blossoming fruit boughs, peach and plum and almond, pear and apple, with the lights and shadows on them from the clouds and snows and mountains, and all those little Tuscan views and landscapes, valleys, olive groves and vineyards, hills crowned with their towns and towers and churches, lifted from the earth, transilluminated there before her eyes.

It was just before they got to Florence that she'd had her moment of rapture, ecstasy, call it what you would, remembering that small Annunciation just as plainly as though she'd stood before it in the Vatican Museum, something about the Virgin's attitude, her hands folded upon her breast and that movement she seemed to be making, a drawing back in awe and denial as though an announcement so great and so astonishing could not by any possibility be true; and the angel, the rush and spread of wings, the garments full and flowing, the hand upraised, had all but overwhelmed her with that sense she'd had of the surpassing mystery, the miracle of birth.

It was just then the door of the compartment opened to let in that ridiculous little courier. What was his name? Fratelli, that was it. "Scusi, scusi," he'd exclaimed, continuing in his nervous, broken, obsequious English. They were nearing Florence, would the ladies permit him to take the luggage from the racks and place it in the corridor? He smiled, and, addressing Cecilia, said that the carriage for Fiesole would be waiting at the station. All the arrangements had been made, the drive in the cool of the evening would be delightful.

"But delightful," he repeated, and, turning to her, expatiated on the joys awaiting her. "When the Signora arrives in Fiesole," he declared, "she will find herself in paradise," and he kissed the ends of his fingers. "But in paradise," he said.

Again the old woman shut her eyes and closed the manuscript. Ah, there was more to it than just the recounting of her quite incredible little tragedy, that laying bare of the secret she had kept through all these years, and which was so faithfully recorded in these pages. It was on the place names now she lingered—Firenze, Fiesole, those months she had spent with the nuns in their convent overlooking Florence. Why, they had a heartscape, a horizon that closed her in with memories which left her vibrating now to an intensity of response entirely unique—to Italy as she'd experienced it at that time of poignant sorrow. To be sure she'd been in Rome but that ancient city had been too large, too crowded with history—the Forum, the Coliseum, the catacombs, St. Peter's and the Vatican, all the Christian churches, dragged hither and thither by Cecilia, telling her about it in her uninformed, irrelevant manner, and her own thoughts but seldom free from her predicament.

But here in the fine weather with the spring rioting wildly in the vineyards and the gardens and the nightingales singing all day long as well as through the night! There had been those drives to Florence down the long hill in the big landau with Fratelli on the box beside the coachman pointing out this sight of interest or the other, and Cecilia next her talking the usual nonsense, the Judas trees in blossom and the wisteria dripping over every wall, passing the contadini in their rattling wine carts, cracking their long whips, shouting their jokes and gay obscenities; then the entrance into the old town, clattering over the cobblestones through the dark streets between the great palaces with their overhanging roofs. And all of a sudden coming out on the Piazza del Duomo, that astonishing display of architecture, the great cathedral with its enormous dome, the baptistry and Giotto's lovely tower intricately overlaid with flowery patterns of mosaic, as though with that happy exuberance of the Renaissance it had been necessary to proclaim in these wondrous structures that this was the city of flowers, the city of youth and renascent spring.

Oh, she couldn't get away from it in Florence, that sense she'd had that one participated in the celebration of life itself, its perpetual renewal. As she scanned the faces of the young women who passed her in the streets and saw their features and expressions again and again repeated in the faces of the Virgins and Madonnas in the churches and museums she became increasingly aware that the masters of the Renaissance had expressed, in their beautiful Annunciations, Nativities, and Assumptions, as much their pagan adoration for life, fertility, as their ecstasy in the presence of the great Christian myths and mysteries. It was here on every side, you couldn't escape it, the declaration of joy in the beauty and mystery of life. She was young and uninstructed historically, and she hadn't so much got it through her intellect as through her senses, through every fiber of her being, so that now she had only to think about that extraordinary time to feel it flowing back to her through all the tides of memory—the language, the voices, the smells, vistas down the long dark streets, sunlight on the palaces, in the piazzas, clattering over the pavements, walking past the monuments. crossing the bridges, going into museums, entering churches.

She had not, of course, been able to have it out with Cecilia. Day after day had passed, keeping up the same old farce, going in and out of Florence like any other pair of avid sightseers; and then, when it grew very warm and she had found it difficult to be so much upon her feet, the sisters had urged her to remain in the convent garden, and Cecilia had sustained them in this advice. Oh yes, she'd said, she must make herself comfortable in the lovely garden and let her do the honors of the town.

EIGHT

Certain memories are never still, thought the old woman. They are like clouds, they move and shift about, they emit their lights and shadows. You suffer them; they come and go and after a while establish a climate, an ambient all their own.

And there had been a trancelike spell about that convent garden which, even as she thought about the anguish she'd suffered there, began to work upon her—sitting day after day in that long chair, the heat intense, the roses blooming, fading away in such profusion that she'd heard the little sound of petals falling through the hedge. The soft petals accumulating under the hedge, that mass of purple iris, the tall buds, and the blossoms standing up like moths above the broken chrysalises, the pigeons walking up and down beneath the cypress trees engaged in ceaseless conversations, the sisters coming on little errands, bringing her this and that—speaking to them, dismissing them, never allowing her reveries to be disturbed, and seeing, while they retreated down the path between the cypress trees, over the edge of the garden wall, floating off and away into the distance of the skyscape and the mountain ranges, the immense, the lovely panorama, with Florence lying below her in the valley of the Arno; asking herself the same insistent questions. Was Lucien informed or was he not? Did he know that she was about to bear his child? Had he allowed himself to be maneuvered by the same powerful hand that moved her puppets with such skill and deliberation? What would happen to her child? And why, why, why had she not been able to have it out with Cecilia?

So the days passed. And then that day, that moment—impelled by the almost suicidal impulse to get up and go to the parapet. Standing there looking down on Florence—the churches, the bridges, the river flowing golden through the plain; and suddenly with no warning, no preparation for it, those sharp pains ripping through her abdomen. It has begun, it has begun, she'd thought, and clutching her side, holding her breath, she'd managed somehow to get back to her seat in the shade, seeing Cecilia, scaring up the pigeons in front of her while behind her they descended in an arch upon the shadows, coming towards her along the path between the cypress trees. How determined she had been not to let her know her labor had begun. She'd braced herself, she'd taken those long deep breaths, and she had vowed that she would play this game of silence to the bitter end. She'd counted one, two, three, four, five, six; and suddenly it was over and there was Cecilia closing her parasol, kissing her lightly on the forehead. "Oh, darling, here you are," she'd said, "how *comfortable* you look." She was on her way to Florence. She wouldn't be long. There was a call that she must make, a most *important* errand. She'd turned and, waving gaily, traveled down the path that led her to the gate in the garden wall as though bent upon angelic business.

How long before the nuns discovered her condition she has not the ghost of an idea. And as for that tragic childbirth, in the big bare room above the valley of the Arno, her labor had been so long and unremitting, the Angelus ringing, and later the same bells ringing for the matin services, that she had never been certain whether it was the call to morning or to evening prayers to which she listened.

Would her anguish never cease? Could it be possible that it was evening—that it was dawn? Was it a feast day? Was it Sunday? In Italy they rang the bells for all the great occasions, for birth and death and burial, and it comforted her to think that they were answering each other across the hills and valleys while she labored with this painful birth, tugging with all the strength remaining to her at the sheer tied to the bedpost, hearing the doctor say *"Coraggio,"* sinking back among the pillows, and in the intervals between the spasms experiencing that extraordinary exaltation. The intervals grew shorter and the pains intolerable. If she listened she could locate the various chimes. A little way down the slope the bells of Settignano. Those nearer, louder, rang in Fiesole, farther down the hill the bells of San Gervaso. Ah, the tolling of the great cathedral bell in Florence and such a curious sense of being lifted up in the moments of exaltation between the brutal spasms, of floating out, drifting away with the church bells, distributing herself among the olive groves and vineyards, of being one with earth, with the processes of life, renascence. If she held to the thought that she was assisting at the greatest of all life's miracles it would help her to be brave, for the pains returned with redoubled violence.

She'd sat up, the sweat beading her forehead, streaming down her face.

She heard the doctor, "Pull, Signora, pull with all your strength."

The sister came with a wet cloth and wiped her face, her hands. "Oi, oi, oi," she'd screamed.

And still the doctor's voice, *"Coraggio."*

"Oi, oi, oi," and the voice of her anguish mingling with the voices of the church bells answering one another with their ancient earthy tongues, and then that sudden stream of sickly sweetish air, breathing it thirstily. Taking another and another breath, the gradual annulment of the torture. And had she or had she not above her exaltation and her anguish heard the doctor saying in Italian, *"Un bel maschio, Signora,"* falling into deep abysses of fatigue and sleep?

And then that rude awakening, thought the old woman, and she moved in her chair and stretched out her arms as though she still implored Cecilia to let her have her child, being to all intents and purposes back again in that cool dim room, the shutters closed against the midday glare—hearing voices drifting through the windows, seeing the sunlight dropped in rungs like a bright ladder tremble on the floor and on the wall against her bed and aware that her cousin looking very fresh and energetic sat beside her—that she was telling her—what was Cecilia telling her? that she looked *so* rested after her refreshing sleep.

She was unable to speak the words—"Where is my baby? I must see my child." They were on her tongue, her heart was bursting with them, but she was listening to Cecilia. What was it Cecilia was saying, prattling on so brightly, stressing certain words and going on with such enthusiasm? "Darling—it's *all* right; it is your grandmother's doing. You must give your grandmother credit for it—that *lovely* couple being here in Florence and at just this moment. Think of it, coming *all* the way from America, the *loveliest* people. I met them by your grandmother's appointment; but the *loveliest* couple, people of excellent family. I am *not* going to tell their name. They want to adopt your little boy, to give him their name and bring him up *exactly* as though he were their own. They have *plenty* of money and they will give him the happiest of lives."

That was word for word exactly what her cousin said. And there she'd lain, paralyzed, unable to speak or move, looking blankly at Cecilia while she went on with further explanations. She had brought the couple up from Florence. There was nothing to do but sign some papers, make some promises, it had all been made *so* simple for her. It was her grandmother that she must thank; all too good to be quite true. Grandmother had managed it with such perfection. She wanted her to stay in Europe for another year. When she returned it would be *exactly* as though nothing had occurred. "Tabula rasa," she had said, repeating the phrase as though she'd coined it.

"Tabula rasa."

Miss Sylvester closed her eyes, and there before her was the angel in the Annunciation she had seen that day upon the train—the rush and spread of wings, the garments full and flowing, the hand upraised.

And then suddenly the poor woman jumped as though she'd been struck a violent and unexpected blow, for the telephone was ringing, stridently demanding her attention. "Dear me," she said, "dear me," and with the greatest difficulty she got up, went to the desk and lifted the receiver from the hook.

NINE

She rose from the telephone and began to pace the room. Dear me, she was highly irritated. Adam was a most exasperating young man, and there was little consistency about her own annoyance since she had been eager to get in touch with him. Now they'd dine tonight together and she could at once discover his address. Capricious enough of him not to have let her have it on the telephone. Where was he living? Oh, he'd said, in a new dump, a hole in the ground below the sidewalk in a street she wouldn't know.

He'd moved, he said, and her supposition about that love affair was, presumably, correct. He was in the bitterest of moods and very exigent about that check he wished to have her cash. She looked at the clock upon her desk. There had been plenty of time for her to have cashed it, if she had wished to do so. Her bank was most accessible, and why she'd been so contrary she didn't know. Surely he could wait until tonight. Down to his last red cent, he'd said. It was his mood had set her off, to say nothing of his having broken into her flow of thought and memory. Well, well, she musn't let her irritation work upon her thus.

It was the way he had responded to her when she spoke to him about the morning's news. It was quite all right by him, the sooner we got blown to Kingdom Come, the better it would be for all concerned.

My God, she said, my God. This world in which we lived, these past decades, unprecedented, unparalleled in history. She had no patience with those who retorted that other ages had been comparable, nothing new or different in this. What utter nonsense! The nightmare of our lives today had no parallel in history. Those monstrous images of terror and the dark, Geryon, Belial, Beelzebub (what were the other names?), prophetic images of evil riding the whirlwind in the Apocrypha, were not to be compared with the shapes that stalked the world today. The skies above our heads were crowded with them, the seas beneath the earth, and in the satanic mills, Los Alamos, Oak Ridge (heavens, there were so many others located who knows where), what shapes, what forms were now materializing. Voices, voices over the air, announcements, appropriations, threats, phantasmagoric images of wars to come. Everyone listening, waiting, and this simultaneity, hearing it together all around the world, shuddering, turning in our sleep, walking through the dream, pure nightmare in which the whole world walked together, pushing the horror down, letting the usual events, the joys and sorrows, the expectations, the personal desires, the vanities and the ambitions, submerge it, hide it deep, deep down, away from our investigation. All in the dream together, every man Jack of us, big fry and little fry alike: and now, for one reason or another, she saw the face of Einstein, its uncanny beauty, the white hair like a halo circling the countenance of a charming, an innocent child. On which of the terrible horses would he be mounted? she wondered, for certainly he rode in the forefront of the procession, along with the politicians, statesmen, the brass hats, the military strategists, and in the rear she saw the rest of the inhabitants of earth, unnumbered, unidentified, running full tilt like so many Gaderine swine, head on for destruction. Mad it was, an insanity unprecedented. Was there in it a self-determined will, a drive towards general, wholesale suicide? No, no, she cried aloud, and again she struck her breast. It was not so, nobody wanted it.

What if, she thought, there could come a moment's pause, everybody ordered to halt, big fry and little fry alike? What if some voice of supreme authority, a voice that could be heard in every corner of the earth, ordained a general pause, a moment's halt in the inexorable procession? What if, in that silence, the wheels of these satanic mills should cease, the voices in the air, the threats and proclamations? If in the silence all could drop upon their knees and pray, pray together for five minutes, give due thought and due consideration to the general madness, might we not somehow or other find that we were saved? But no, we didn't dare, we hadn't the nerve to look it in the face; the only thing was to prepare for it, to accelerate the procession. That seemed to be the great idea. This side and that side of the curtain that divided the world into two opposing camps, the monstrous, the subhuman mechanizations, materializations continued, the whole world geared to the wholesale production of death. Once more the old woman put her hands before her face. Was she trying to drive away the pictures that came into her mind, or was she attempting to visualize them? They staggered the imagination.

No wonder that Adam shrugged his shoulders and asked her why she got so worked up about it all, intimating by his voice and his expression that since she was so soon to exit from the scene forever, there was no need for such agitation. "Well, it matters to me," she said aloud, "it matters more than anything" and again she seemed to be engaged in one of those endless arguments that she carried on with the young man. He belonged, in his surly, stubborn manner, to the wars-have-always-been-and-always-will-be school of thinking. He liked to quote history and trot out his greater knowledge to confound her. Nothing different in the human situation, only on a larger scale—that he would concede, the scale of it. He was a Spenglerian and used to quote those passages about the great Khans and the epochs soon to dawn upon us, the bigger and the better wars about to come. It was apparent enough to her that he was sick to death of the whole dreadful subject. Had he not, poor boy, seen enough of it already, waiting there in France for them to soften up the enemy's resistance, and later marching into Germany over the Remagen bridge, and seeing the wreck and ruin of all those bombed-out cities?

What the eyes of the young men had seen, the abhorrent scenes, the pictures pushed down into the deepest wells of memory; and hereupon she began enumerating the great terrains of battle, islands in the Pacific, the beachheads, the battles in the desert. She too had seen them, comfortably seated in her armchair, at the movie theaters; but to imagine it, the nerves, the senses—eyes, ears, the shuddering flesh exposed. It was a marvel to her that so many of them still preserved their sanity. No wonder they challenged the years to come with the supreme insolence of disregard.

No wonder that Adam was disconcerted and irritated when she dwelt upon it with such persistency. He was determined to snatch eagerly, hungrily at all that he could get, living on so little, attempting to complete his education, and writing of course that novel which devoured him. The moment was pregnant with possibilities. Was her interest in Adam, she asked herself, a kind of substitution? He was the same age as that young man she would never lay her eyes on, stamped with the imprint of the same horrendous years. More than likely he too had been flung out into one or another of the outrageous areas. Perhaps his bones were bleaching on the Libyan desert. Maybe he was lying under a nameless cross on some island in the Pacific. It might be—and this seemed to her more right—that his dust was scattered among the vineyards and the hills of Italy.

Well, the less she thought of him, that child to whom she had so rashly decided to leave the bulk of her fortune, the better for her state of mind. Anonymity was, when she reflected upon it, a condition she should now be willing to accept. Had she not kept her secrets to herself, and was there a soul alive to care whether she had a past or not? Anonymous she was, and somehow always had been.

Anonymous was the word for the lot of us, she thought, as she continued to gaze at the accustomed view, the office buildings with their bright panes reflecting the scudding clouds, and behind the windows countless men and women in their busy cells. She seemed to see the entire world, the human hive collapsing, falling in upon itself, the integuments melting, disappearing, cities, insolent skyscrapers falling, falling. The bees swarmed; the cities fell, and, attempting to blot out the dreadful pictures fringing her imagination, she remembered how she had read, she didn't know exactly where, that, measured against the aeons, the endless procession of evolving species, the birds were practically new arrivals on the stage of life, and how it had pleased her to call them little John the Baptists, singing in the wilderness, prophesying, preaching the gospel of one to come, the latchet of whose shoes they were not worthy to unloose.

Ridiculous, she thought, for Adam to assert so stubbornly that this age did not in basic experiences differ from the other ages. It was the simultaneity of our responses to the catastrophes, what with the very waves of air transporting us, riding us round the habitable globe, photographs flowing through space, and voices, voices. Try to press the pictures and the voices down, to hide them in the deepest wells of the subconscious. The world was too much with us, it had entered the secret, the most uneasy placing of being—conscience.

And here we were, hawking our souls about, writing novels, our own little autobiographies (all the novels were, in one way or another, autobiographical), young and old alike engaged in it, dissecting, anatomizing, breaking up the moments, and there was something not to be passed over lightly in the startling fact that the splitting of the atom and the splitting of the soul, the long, long range of human memory, had been contemporaneous, all in the open world together, no shelter for us, no place to hide. And suddenly there was a poem upon her lips, she couldn't for the life of her remember where she'd read it, but the words seemed, as she recited them, the very voice of her apprehension.

"Put out the stars an instant, Lord,
Lest all these swords and scimitars
Frighten this snail who goes abroad
For the first time without his mail.
Behold him laid along the slim
Green blade of grass too frail for him.
He has no home, no church, no dome
To shelter him. He goes alone.
Put out the stars an instant, Lord,

Lest all these swords and scimitars
Turn him to stone."

She repeated the last two lines, and found to her astonishment that she was standing in the center of the room, attempting to collect her wits.

What had she intended to do? She must get herself some lunch. Stepping rather unsteadily into the bathroom, she looked about her. Here was a can of soup, here were biscuits, there on the windowsill was fruit. When she'd had something to eat she'd get back to her chair and go on with that manuscript to the bitter end.

But where, where in the world was the can opener? She searched frantically among the queer utensils under the tub. It was these wretched little gadgets she felt unable to contend with.

BOOK 2

ONE

It was a clear evening. Miss Sylvester stood at the window. She had finished her manuscript and she sighed heavily. Her novel had left her with a feeling of incredulity occasioned not so much by the fact that her story savored of the unusual, if not to say the melodramatic, as by the positively imponderable strangeness of the human condition, one's existing in this world at all. There was something about this winter hour when the lights were bright in all the assembled windows which never failed to impress her as entirely unreal, especially if as was the case tonight a small slice of the wintry moon could be seen sailing round the corner of the Metropolitan Tower.

She had told the story of her life and, she must admit it, it had moved her profoundly—left her as novels frequently did with a residue of emotion that she often carried in her heart for some time after she had finished them. But oddly enough she was irritated that this was so. If her book should fall into the hands of others addicted as she was to the habitual reading of novels, what exactly would their feeling be? Doubtless they would regard her history as a very tragic one indeed. Poor girl, or more likely poor unfortunate woman, they'd think, what a sad time she'd had of it, and would they not be liable to carry away from the perusal of her book something of the same soft and not unpleasant ache of love and sympathy that she felt herself for her poor heroine?

Well, well, she reflected, peering at the young moon and the incredible citadels of light as though in the face of such a spectacle it was something of an impertinence to indulge oneself in personal tragedy at all. New York had been her home for over fifty years, nearly three-quarters of her life. Think of the changes, think of the events! Why, on her first arrival she had lived only a few blocks north on Fifth Avenue. All these neighboring streets had looked considerably like the Back Bay—low three-story houses with high stoops, maids at windows pulling down the blinds, front doors opening to let in children and nursemaids, ladies in long skirts alighting from carriages, gentlemen with canes and top hats walking down the stoops. Very decorous and stable, more or less rooted in tradition, no intimation of this neon-lighted metropolis hung crazily in air, people inhabiting a few cubic feet of sky and regarding it a valid piece of real estate.

Taking up the manuscript and holding it as though she weighed it in her hands, the old woman reseated herself. Book One, she said aloud, Book Two. Yes, that had been, she thought, an excellent device—skipping all those years, giving but short shrift to that anguish, that complete death of the heart (the year in Europe with Cecilia, her return to Brookline, her final severance from family ties), and placing her heroine, after nearly two decades of residence in New York, there on Fifth Avenue in that memorable parade. And she'd achieved it admirably, looping up into a single chapter the thoughts and resolutions with their backward and their forward glances, and setting her novel in motion again on that tide of faith in human nature and the future of the race. That had seemed to her on that May afternoon to have reached its highest flood, loosed as it had been from the hearts of all those men and women walking up the avenue. With Mary Morton at her side and that group of Italian working women she had browbeaten into taking their part in the great demonstration forming a small battalion, she had asked herself if it was possible in a world where there was so much human misery, so many wrongs to right, for one woman to cling tenaciously to her own particular griefs. Today I turn my back upon the sorrows I have known, I shall forget my past. Those were the words to which she'd set her feet to marching and, with the band only a few sections ahead of her playing almost exclusively as she recalls it "The Battle Hymn of the Republic," "Mine eyes have seen the glory of the coming of the Lord," getting the rhythms of her body somehow or other swung into the rhythms, not of the familiar words, but of her own brave resolutions, she had been borne buoyantly on and up the avenue.

Ah, thought the old woman, we are inclined to laugh whenever we see the pictures of those old processions. What funny hats we wore, those high collars, the long skirts that swept the ankles, the stance of all those standard bearers, the resolution in those faces, all that seriousness, that dedication. But if the world could recapture it again, that buoyancy and hope, all that faith and optimism, the protest against injustice, inhumanity, the comradeship, the pledging and resolving, the banding together in unity and friendliness which somehow or other on that particular afternoon had joined and gathered to a tide. It spread along the line of march, it communicated itself from heart to heart, that sense one had that the world was getting better, that new visions and concepts were abroad. She remembers what joy she had experienced thinking of the splendid women marching with her in the same procession, of the distinguished men who had laid themselves open to the jeers and insults of the crowd to march along with them in this demonstration of their strength. Everyone, she'd thought, with vision and with courage is out today rejoicing in a common faith—a belief in the future of the world. There was a spirit in the air she could not well define, participation, comradeship—joy at being alive and able to consider oneself a useful member of society. So on and up the avenue behind the bands and banners she had marched, making her own brave resolutions, embarking as it seemed to her upon a new life, a good life.

In the beauty of the lilies Christ was born across the sea. Today I turn my back upon the sorrows I have known, I shall forget my past. As though one could forget one's past, exclaimed the old woman, looking up to see that there rested on the Metropolitan Tower and on those citadels of life insurance at the foot of the avenue the cool bright glow of winter twilight. You might as well tell a river to stop flowing as to say to anybody, now forget your past. Your past was contained within you, a part of this moment or the next; the scent of a flower, the song of a bird, music as you entered a room, some sight on which your eyes were resting, and back it rushed into the mind again—as though she had not been all the way up Fifth Avenue, even while she was saying those brave words, swinging her body into the rhythms of that glorious hymn, remembering her past, passing this landmark or that, and finally halting with her little band of working girls directly in front of the house that had actually been her first home in New York. Somewhat washed up it had looked to her, with the shops to the right and left of it, and offering quite a different appearance to its aspect in 1895 when, just one of many similar mansions presenting their high stoops and brownstone fronts to the avenue, it had offered her shelter and refuge from her misery. There she'd waited, standing first on one foot and then on the other, telling herself so gallantly that she was on this day to turn a leaf in her book of life, and the associations rushing over her, mixing and mingling with the memories of those early days in New York, the distressful remembrance of the two years that had followed her return from Europe.

Awful had been that return to Brookline, not indeed as she had imagined it with Lucien in the picture and having to pretend that nothing had happened between them, none of that anticipated agony which she had told herself a hundred times a day she could not face, never a sight of Lucien. She had passed him on the ocean. He and Eleanor were off on an extended trip. And all this dropped casually into the conversation a few hours after her arrival and just as though it held but little interest for her. They would not return for several years. "Your uncle has developed an extraordinary interest in Chinese pottery (or is it temples, Horace?)" her grandmother had elucidated. "Your Uncle Lucien is," she'd continued, "a very cultivated man." And with this to make him as inaccessible as possible she changed the subject quite abruptly. Life went on. Lucien never again made an appearance, driving out from Boston as in the old days to make those sudden calls that had always furnished her with so much joy. He never appeared on Sundays for the usual midday dinners. No sight or sound of him. And when the time came finally to go to The Towers that was what she had not been able to endure. Why, she'd almost died of it. The less she thought about it now the better, being there where every scent and sound and sight had brought the memories back so swiftly, lying awake at night and listening to the waves and always trying to stop the words from coming (they were a portion of the very breath she drew), "You are part of all things great and quiet, my beloved." She hadn't cared what happened to her, and returning for her second Brookline winter she'd simply allowed life to be taken out of her own hands altogether. She'd become the victim not only of nervous prostration but of a romantic and disastrous love affair which it was presumed she had sustained while traveling in Europe. Toted about from doctor to doctor, listening with complete apathy to that astonishing array of lies and allusions, and finding her life embellished by a romance quite different from the sorrow which consumed her, she had paid no attention to the advice of the doctors or the stern admonitions of her grandmother. She must take an interest in life, she must go out into society, she must find some kind of a hobby, she must stop reading so much. She had made it her deliberate business to pine away, cherishing a vague hope that, like the heroine of the romance trumped up around her, she might presently die of a broken heart.

And then suddenly when life was at its very lowest ebb her grandmother had in her desperation brought out of the unknown and the unsuspected into the very forefront of those plans and decisions as to what in the world to do with her next that neglected and forgotten, that impoverished relative, Miss Leonie Lejohn, who had turned her pleasant home on Fifth Avenue into a very select and suitable board-inghouse. Leonie should chaperon her. There could be no better place to send her than to New York. It developed too that she was to take up singing. She had had a father who had played the flute, her voice was very pleasing, she had an excellent ear, it was not unlikely that she could develop a genuine talent for music. And so, subscribing as apathetically to the scheme as to any of the other prescriptions for the condition of her soul, almost before she knew what it was all about she had found herself at Cousin Leonie's.

For once, she'd said to herself, getting into line and step and casting a backward glance at the high stoop, the brownstone façade still standing there amid the shops and restaurants, her grandmother had struck it right, she'd made the perfect choice. There'd been something about it, something, and breathing again the smell of asphalt, that smell of the Avenue in the nineties, hearing again the vast rumble of vehicles, carriage wheels, cart wheels, and the descent of horses' hooves, plunk, plunk in the asphalt, she'd lived through it all again, stepping out of a morning with the large impersonal roar of the great city in her ears and that sense within her, though she wouldn't for the world allow herself to acknowledge that she felt it, that she was still young, that life had an interest, a positive fascination for her. And how extraordinary it is, she thought, keeping step, keeping step, He is trampling out the vineyards where the grapes of wrath are stored, the vitality, the recuperative power of youth, just being there in New York with her talent flowering and blossoming, how exciting it had seemed, with Eva Winters (yes, there had been poor Eva, what a part she'd played in all of it), Eva, whose passion for music equaled her own and whose voice had been not much better or maybe not much worse than hers, and who, if she cared to take a backward glance, had probably put into the head of Cousin Leonie in her correspondence with her grandmother the idea that singing lessons might be the best anodyne to apply to a heart that was almost at the point of breaking. She and Eva had had at any rate the same singing master, Signor Vittorio Locatelli, who raved with almost equal fervor about the voices of both talentless pupils. Under the inspiration of the fiery-eyed little maestro what a passionate enthusiasm for music they'd each of them worked up. Music-crazed they'd been, starting off together in the earliest hours of daylight to procure for themselves if possible seats in the very front row of that topmost, neck-breaking, back-breaking gallery of the Metropolitan. What Wagnerians they became. To hear "The Ring" again and still again as many times as it was given, that had been their idea of bliss, sitting there imagining themselves impersonating those famous heroines, Isolde, Brünnehilde. Strange, exotic had been those agonies, intensities, resting her chin upon the rail of that uncomfortable "nigger heaven," while the music pouring from the lighted pit and the stage so far below became not so much the score of Wagner as the inexhaustible stream of emotion welling from her agitated heart. She'd swooned, she'd swayed, she'd practically melted away in an ecstasy of remembrance and delectable indulgence in her grief, and, let her admit it now, even while she'd thrown herself with complete abandon into the splendid agonies of those majestic heroines, she'd been quite well aware that Eva, who she knew to have heard the legend of that fictitious heart-breaking European love affair, was watching with the keenest awe and interest the spectacle of her abandonment to grief. For there had been, she must confess it, much sweetness in holding in her gift and even while she kept her secret locked within her breast the sympathy which at that period everyone was so ready to bestow upon her, and although she knew, with that habit of silence long built up in her, that her story would not be whispered to a soul on earth, she had felt enormous satisfaction in being pointed out and noticed as a creature so young and so afflicted.

Fantasy, catharsis, call it what you would, a necessary phase perhaps, a way in which she'd learned to find her grief endurable. Glamorous, exciting it had been walking among the crowds on those enchanted New York pavements, living in her cloud of dreams. And so, swinging along in time with the brave resolutions (today I turn my back upon the sorrows I have known), continuing in step with her beloved Mary, she'd rehearsed it marching up the avenue.

TWO

Well, if she had to say it, thought the old woman, that had been quite a tour de force. She'd done it very well indeed getting her heroine all the way to the Plaza and trailing the memories along with her, the story so clearly told and the scenes so vividly rendered. None the less there had been something omitted. Suddenly she began to beat her breast with the familiar emphasis. Something felt, here in the heart and along the channels of the blood, a sweetness, a quickness, some suppressed excitement, why those early years in New York had had a pulse-beat entirely their own and, she'd have to acknowledge some surprise in the realization of this, they had been thoroughly pleasurable, delightful. The flow and rhythm of one's life could not be communicated. It was carried here. Again she pounded her breast, here in the heart.

How could she possibly describe that house of Leonie's—it was all in entering the front door, walking up the long flight of stairs to her room, passing that bronze statue of the Venus de Milo in the niche at the curve of the stairs, getting that sniff of escaping gas, old carpets and ancient plumbing in the hall, stopping as she entered her big sepulchral room and before turning on the gas to listen to the roar and rumble outside. Nothing so exciting as that had ever met her ears, the loud, the assertive voice of New York, whispering to herself that she was here on her own, leading her own life. Something about it, that extraordinary domicile, that had from the beginning spelled adventure, the front rooms looking out upon the avenue and that endless procession of vehicles, the horses' feet descending, prancing up and down the pavement plunk, plunk, plunk.

There was the faded shabby elegance of the long drawing room and, at the back, the other side of the folding doors, the long dark dining room which constituted the stage and center of that fascinating drama—life as it was led at Cousin Leonie's. The long table always covered with a white cloth, changed each Sunday and stained with many grease spots towards the end of every week. Cousin Leonie dispensing coffee from a large old-fashioned urn at breakfast and soup from a large china tureen at dinner, toying delicately with the teacups at the luncheon hour ("One lump, Mr. Langley?" "A dash of cream, Miss Playfair?"), doing her level best to keep up the tone of her establishment and Mr. Langley on her right doing more than his best to support her endeavor—a funny eccentric little man with a waxed mustache and very shiny trousers. Interested in genealogy, he spent most of his time at the public libraries investigating family trees. Cousin Leonie had a perfect genius for knowing without having to study it up exactly who of any importance was connected with whom, so that conversation, if the two of them had their way, consisted entirely in enumerating and recapitulating names. Then there was Miss Playfair who, they used to intimate, was a mere parvenue. She kept her own little brougham and inhabited the largest room in the house. She tried to make it out that Miss Leonie's was her own residence, and was driven to the oddest expedients in explaining to her visitors the intrusion upon her private scene of such a queer assortment of characters. Last and least of all was Mrs. Canfield. Supported by a small group of friends and relatives whose monthly subscriptions made it possible for her to inhabit a tiny hall bedroom on the top floor and to enjoy three meals a day, she regarded it a privilege to breathe the air surrounding her, and was always saying "Dear me," or "Yes," or "No" at what seemed to her the appropriate moment. Offsetting, spellbinding, disconcerting and generally discombobulating all these odd had-beens and would-be's were Mary Morrison and her queer friend Morty (Mr. Martin Morton, as Miss Leonie never failed to call him).

Ah how vividly she could see dear Mary now, that face, the cloud of dark hair around it, and the black eyes that seemed to give off a kind of sulphurous smoke, the nose broken at the bridge, and that glow of health and vitality, as though somehow or other her love of life and her interest in it had been gathered right up into her countenance, where it gave off its warmth and glow like a hearth at which the sick and the self-centered could come to warm themselves. How passionately Mary loved the fullness and variety of life, how passionately she loved the world, and with what eagerness she dedicated herself to reforming it, for making it better, as she used to say, for the next generation to live in. She could not sit down at that table without knocking the proprieties and absurdities and conventions into a cocked hat. She discarded conventions, she discarded all the rules and orders of her day. She'd been, she had to acknowledge it, pretty appalled by Mary at first, and though fascinated, fascinated, had tried to stand out against her. All her recklessness and daring, all her scholarship and seriousness, with none of her warmth and humor and humanity impaired. And what a mind she had. A woman with a mind like that!—taking all those courses, reading all those books, a freak, a wonder, a phenomenon. And with the eager, the factual, the estimable Morty so head over heels in love with her that the rooms the two of them inhabited together positively rocked and shook with what, they made no bones about it, appeared to be going on between them. What commotion her very presence in their midst incurred.

The way Mary used to air her opinions. How she liked to shock, astonish, always bringing the underprivileged into the discussions, and her belief in trade unions. What other weapons had the poor industrial workers but their collective strength? she'd ask. And she'd usually turn to Miss Playfair. Did she have any idea of the conditions under which the clothes she had on her back were manufactured? No, she'd bet she didn't. And Miss Playfair turning a very cold shoulder would try to incite Mrs. Canfield's indignation, the poor bewildered little lady nodding her head or shaking it as she thought most expedient, muttering "Dear me," "Yes," "No," "I never did," and Mr. Langley who knew every root and branch of Mary's family tree (was she not a Morrison, one of *the* Morrisons?) expressing unutterable consternation, looking at Miss Leonie as though to implore her to show Mary the front door at once.

With Eva there was something else—jealousy. Eva had somehow sensed from the first that there was a kind of kinship between herself and Mary. "I don't like her," she'd say, "she frightens me. I don't see how you can be so fascinated by her. I think she's dreadful." She'd denied it. No, she'd said, she wasn't fascinated. But Eva had guessed it right. She'd loved her from the first. However, it had taken that friendship a long time to declare itself; and it caused her the profoundest remorse to remember how when Mary used to say to her, "Come along with Morty and me to one of our meetings," she'd sneak out after dinner hoping nobody had seen her go with them. The meetings were dreary enough in all conscience, held in smoky rooms and among what had seemed to her the most unrefined and unattractive people. There they'd sit, smoking, discussing, organizing, and Mary and Morty so familiar with them. Pretty lacking in glamor it had been when she compared it to the hours spent in Eva's company at the Metropolitan.

Poor Miss Leonie was rather at her wits' end, for Mary's mother was an old friend and she'd promised to keep an eye on the wayward girl. She kept the place in perpetual ferment. Miss Playfair was always declaring ultimatums, "Either I go or they depart." Such a pair endangered the repute of the house. Why, Mr. Morton visited Mary in her room. They smoked cigarettes together! It was an outrage. As for her effect on the other young women in her charge, well, that was Miss Leonie's lookout. If she didn't write to Miss Sylvester's grandparents she would undertake to do so herself.

Finally Mary and Morton solved all the problems by simply lighting out together one fine day in the second winter after her arrival. Heavens, what a to-do. Miss Playfair made a big scandal out of it even though the first thing they'd done on leaving was to go directly to a justice of the peace—imagine it. She wouldn't give a snap of her finger for such a marriage. They were living in open sin, and a good thing it was for Miss Leonie, bringing down the repute of her house and everybody in it by keeping such a pair beneath her roof. But gracious, how sadly she and all the rest of them had missed dear Mary. Nobody to shock and scandalize, to make the very breath of life begin to circulate around that stuffy dinner table. Even Eva felt at a loss, having to listen every night to Miss Leonie and Mr. Langley exchange genealogical data, putting up with Miss Playfair's pretensions and Mrs. Canfield's subservience.

And as for herself there had been a hollow in her heart—that suppressed anticipation at the thought of seeing Mary every night at dinner now extinguished. There had been the queerest void. Even her music began to wear a trifle thin. An intimation that there was in Mary's gift something that might stand her in better stead than that very reedlike voice about which Signor Locatelli raved so extravagantly began to announce itself as actual fact. How she had missed her! And when she turned up one evening with Morty and invited her to go out with them, "Come along with us on a spree," what joy she'd felt! How exhilarating she had found it to brave everybody's disapproval and start boldly off with them. That was the night that dated for her the actual beginning of their long and steadfast friendship, that sense that Mary'd had of her as of a poor benighted creature in need of just exactly what she had to offer somehow declared itself that winter night—it became a warmth within her, sweetness, joy.

For who can say, thought the old woman. The love that fills our hearts has its tides and overflows mysteriously, disperses itself in so many and such varying channels. One's passion for art, for nature, beauty; and always, always that feeling one has for life itself with its insatiable hungers, its overwhelming sympathies. And if she must confess it at this late hour of her life, with all the central founts of love—sexual passion and maternity—so disastrously cut off, had not this deep, this steadfast friendship for Mary been the one human relationship where love had never failed to nourish and replenish her?

The spree on which they went consisted in going to the slums. "We're taking you into the ghetto," Mary explained. Ah, that was a night she had not so much as mentioned in her novel. How could she have done so? Too swift, too fluid in the memory the scenes and the emotions—that sense she'd had walking between her friends, arm linked in arm, that there were being opened up for exploration large and hitherto unimagined areas of life. Grand Street, Division Street, Delancey. A cold night with occasional flurries of snow and the blue flames from the small acetylene lamps that dimly and intermittently lighted the pushcarts and the faces of the crowds blown off into the wind like birds, like flowers. Such crowds, such an assemblage of strange peoples teeming, pullulating, boiling over, the pushcarts drawn up in a double line on either side of the curb, the dark mass of the tenements looming up to right and left—that feeling she had had of being closed in by tenements stretching off in solid blocks to north and south and east and west—multitudes out that winter night haggling, bargaining, pushing—the laden carts displaying every variety of merchandise—hairpins, shoestrings, pickles, aprons, dresses, bars of nougat, kitchen utensils, mounds of nuts, rugs, linoleum, fruits; Mary explaining, "It's the bazaar, the ghetto." The bazaar it was, the ghetto, but something else that teased the mind, ancient, Biblical— those faces, the pushcart vendors with their eyes rapt back on some fixed point of meditation and their beards blown in the wind— Isaiah, Jeremiah, Abraham; fish for sale, ribbons, vegetables, children's apparel—the vigor of those women, their grasp and strife and surge, the large deep-breasted mothers of the race sorting, bargaining, picking over the merchandise, jostling you off the sidewalks, milling round with their indomitable vigor; Mary beside her, "No room for all these people, look at the tenements, see the homes we give our immigrants—in they come, thousands by the month"; Morty waving a vague hand in the direction of the harbor, "That's our industrial civilization for you." Mary, who had told her in a whispered conversation on the streetcar that she and

Morty were going to have a child, warm, well clad against her arm, "You should see these streets in daylight. You should go inside some of these tenements. You wait, I'll take you with me, I'll show you children. What our industrial civilization does to children. I'll show you mothers. You wait, I'll take you with me," showing life to her, trying to sell sympathy to her, to sell love to her, to give her you might say the whole wide world to take into her arms, the wind blowing and the snow increasing and the blue flames caught in the wind like birds, like flowers, and memory bringing to her mind remembrance of that early dawn in the big room overlooking Florence, that sense she'd had of distributing herself among the vineyards and the orchards. Had Mary maybe got some inkling of the nature of her grief? Between them there had been something, a sympathy as though with her quick intuitions she had guessed or very nearly guessed her secret.

That then had been the real beginning of her long and remarkable friendship, her association with Mary in her work and interests. The shifting of allegiances, abandoning Eva and Locatelli for the great business of trying to reform the world, had of course been gradual, but Mary and Morton had seemed bent on introducing her to the sufferings of the poor. They wished to have her see it at firsthand, to actually get it as they used to say "circulating in the mind, in the imagination, a part of the heart's blood," and it was in connection with that branch of her own work dearest to her heart, the attempt then being made to do away with industrial processes carried on in the tenements, that Mary got her first to visiting the homes where children, little boys and girls scarcely more than babies, were kept all day long at unimaginable tasks.

Loading dice, finishing coats and pants, making willow plumes, artificial flowers. Ah, she could see those children now, clad in scanty clothing, eyes dulled with mortal weariness, little hands and minds conditioned to the various coordinations. There in those bare kitchens she used to find them, their eyes mirroring only what they saw reflected in the eyes of the driven, the exploiting parent—fear, urgency, hunger, terrified by the intrusion, looking up like frightened beasts. Afraid of what—of penalization, punishment? In all those eyes, the mother eyes, the dull eyes of the children, the same expression, as of souls already killed, creatures already thrown upon the waste heap, finished, exploited to the very last shred of human endurance.

And so, one thing leading to another, she had finally become a part of that great movement, the stirring in the hearts of men and women, at the turn of the century, of indignation at the evils of society, that hope in human nature, the belief that it was capable of improvement, the desire to right the wrongs, to make the world as Mary used to say with head thrown back and sudden fire in her eyes a better place in which to live. She had found the right, the perfect occupation, and presently she'd had a stroke of luck, she'd become the beneficiary of a will. Let no one ever tell her that money contributed but little to the enjoyment of life. Why, when she'd found herself with money of her own, dependent on nobody, capable of making her own choices, doing what she wished with what she had, it had made all the difference in the world. All so unexpected too, her grandfather dying suddenly and his fortune entailed to be divided, left in equal parts to his children and their issue, and as both aunts were childless there she was at twenty-eight with a decent little fortune of her own, the income to be hers till she was thirty and after that the entire principal hers to squander as she pleased. Good luck it was indeed, let no one say it wasn't. No time at all before she'd bade goodbye to Cousin Leonie's—egged on by Mary ("What, wait and let your grandmother dictate to you what your life is going to be—with all that money yours. I never heard of such a thing"), she'd made her declaration of independence; she'd taken an apartment not far from Mary and Morton. She'd walked breast to breast with them in all their plans and leagues and projects.

And so on that fine afternoon in May 1915 life had seemed to her a pretty glorious affair. It had been good to her, it had given her Mary and all these Italian working girls marching along with her, keeping step, keeping step. Today I turn my back upon the sorrows I have known. I shall forget my past.

THREE

Well, it had been only a few days after that parade that the past had come barging up at her in the most extraordinary manner. The curious thing about it had been that she'd recognized the fact the moment she'd held that blue heavily-scented envelope in her hand. Eleanor, she'd thought, looking at the Boston postmark, recognizing the handwriting. Opening it, seeing the gold monogram with the crest above it, enveloped by the still familiar scent—heavens, her aunt might have been in the room with her—she'd read the little missive, large letters scrawled across the page with a great many words heavily underlined. "My *darling* little niece, it's so many years since you and Lucien and I have seen each other. We shall be in New York Saturday next staying at the Plaza—and *will* you come at four-thirty to have a cup of tea with us? We *must* hear all about you. We *suppose* that you are quite a songstress now."

How upset she'd been, put out of her stride all day. Why revive those memories, she'd asked herself, and during that interminable committee meeting and amid the endless discussion she'd resolved many times that she would not go; she'd changed her mind as frequently—since the request had come from Eleanor why and for what reason could she possibly say no? Tortured by indecision she had not answered till the following day when she'd written the briefest possible reply—yes, she'd be there. It would be nice to see them again. In the interval she'd wondered why in heaven's name she had not turned her back on the proposal (the old unanswered questions had pursued her. How much had Eleanor known? How much had been kept from her? Did Lucien know about the child?), and when she'd come to dress for the appointment how undecided she had been about her costume. Should she look her dowdiest and simply rub it in that she had turned her back upon the world of foolishness and fashion or would she wear her new spring clothes? She was forty-nine. That was, if anyone asked her opinion, the moment when a woman was at her very prime. She'd scrutinized her face with care. She was not by any means a beauty like Aunt Eleanor but still she had her points. She'd made up her mind that she would look her best.

She'd been early for the appointment and had gone into the park and sat down on one of the green benches close to the entrance, pretty appalled at being there at all and rather inclined to get up and go directly home. The day was perfectly lovely and she remembers how she had looked with the tenderest affection at the flowers of the maple trees, yellow and red, crushed on the pavement by the feet of the passersby, and then up through the boughs above her head, deep, deep into the blue sky between the leaves thinking how perfectly exquisite they were—the leaves and buds and blossoms spread out like flowers in water on the air.

She was pervaded by the spring, that sense of being still endowed with youth—the same old heart in ferment. And suddenly dropping her eyes she'd seen emerging from the mists and all the lacy greenery and in the procession of the other vehicles about to leave the park (it could not be, she thought, yes, it certainly was)

Aunt Eleanor and Lucien Grey. There they sat behind the chauffeur in that high landau with the top thrown back, Eleanor grown a great deal stouter, dressed with extreme elegance, and Lucien still slender, wearing a Homburg hat in the jauntiest possible manner, about them both something unmistakably European as though an afternoon drive and in exactly those lazy, lolling attitudes had become the habitual order of their days.

No, she thought, I can't go on with it; why should I? But even while she said it getting up. How weak she'd felt, her knees shaking under her. Trying to keep her eyes on them, she crossed the street, saw the car swing round the Plaza and stop in front of the hotel. There seemed to be some delay about their getting out and she'd had ample time to watch Eleanor while Lucien assisted her to get out of the car. How stout she'd grown, florid, and her hair, no question about it, dyed that startling copper-gold. And Lucien, dear me, dear me, it was all in the way he moved, the way he helped, handled her, you might say, as though assisting her in and out of cars and carriages, trailing behind her into dining rooms, picking up her handkerchiefs had become (where had they been? What had they done with themselves all these years?) the chief business of his life. They gave their orders to the chauffeur, dismissed him, and stood an instant on the sidewalk looking vaguely out across the Plaza. Then just as they were about to turn and go into the hotel Eleanor caught sight of her and coming forward with her arms outstretched, "My darling little niece," she drew it out affectionately. Pressed against that ample bosom, positively drenched in the somehow familiar odor of her perfumes, she felt herself kissed first on one cheek and then on the other, conscious all the time that Lucien was standing there beside her. Eleanor let her go and turned to him. "Why, Lucien," she drawled, "she hasn't changed a bit."

Lucien came forward. Would he kiss her or would he not? Good God, he extended his hand, he took one of her hands, lifted it to his mouth, kissed the back of her white glove. "Margaret," he said, and she might have been wrong but it seemed to her his voice was shaking, "Margaret, let me look at you."

All three started up the steps, went on into the hotel, Lucien regaining his savoir faire (if indeed he'd lost it), tripping round her with considerable agility in his endeavor to assist Eleanor who was a bit unsteady on her feet. Thus the three of them walked through the spacious airy hall (she could never go into the Plaza through that particular door without reenacting the entire scene), she and Lucien in the wake of the large, beautiful, perfectly possessed woman drawling out her little questions and comments as though they'd been the only people in the place. Would they like to have tea in the little or the big dining room? What an extraordinary hotel, so large and *American*. "Look, Lucien, at those absurd jardinieres."

Miraculous at moments are the powers of insight, the ability to put this suddenly with that. Certain it is that in those four or five minutes, trailing along behind Eleanor and with the oddest feeling that the spring, the green trees outside, all that movement of boughs and the passing of vehicles was somehow still a part of the poignant experience, seating herself (they finally decided to have tea in the little dining room) at a small, prettily-appointed table and a great to-do about who should order tea and who should take chocolate in process, she appeared to have found an answer to many of the questions that had so tortured and bewildered her throughout the years.

Lucien had, there was no doubt of it in her mind, even while enjoying with her their delightful secret interchange, even while bored to death by all the banality and repetition of the family scenes, belonged to that world of Chamberlains and Fosters—he had been tied and bound to it hand and foot. She had watched him push back Eleanor's chair, rearrange her scarf, had noticed she remembers that he carried in his pocket a small French novel and even while she was attempting to make out the title on the cover she'd got it all in an astounding flash, her mind traveling back with the most extraordinary conviction to the moment that held for her the clue to her bewilderment—that morning at the breakfast table when Lucien had announced so suddenly that he and Eleanor were leaving for the mountains. For what she'd seen again was Eleanor, that look she'd worn upon her face—sensual, possessive, triumphant. It was Eleanor who'd forced the issue. Ah, she had known, this dull, this repetitious woman, what was hers to give and to retract. She had taken her shrewd and well-calculated risk there as they'd lain beside each other in the summer night, for about that seldom if ever mentioned word, which more than likely had at that time never so much as passed her lips, Eleanor had known all there was to know. He should choose between the two of them. That's exactly what she'd told him, not with anger but with all the persuasiveness of her beauty, her passion, and her desire; he could go on with it if he wished to, but he must face the music out alone.

"Darling, would you like tea or chocolate? The chocolate here is perfectly delicious. Let me recommend it," she'd prattled on, treating her exactly as though she were taking a child off on a spree.

However, her attention was immediately distracted. The Plaza did not provide the kind of tea that Lucien preferred. There was conversation among the waiters, the headwaiter ran up. "Your Uncle Lucien," she explained, "since his visit to China, has become a connoisseur of teas." "Let it go, let it go," Lucien said, noticeably put out. And as she watched them she had seen a series of small tableaus taking place in hotels and restaurants all over the continent of Europe, waiters rushing up with wine lists, waiters hovering over menus, for what they ate and what they drank had become a matter of the greatest moment to this childless pair. "We should have gone as you suggested to the St. Regis," said Eleanor. Stealing a glance at Lucien, Margaret had done her best to make what she could out of it all. No, he had not changed too much, grown older of course, and he was rather stooped, but there was still a look of distinction about him, the same fine features and that plasticity about the molding of the face under the cheekbones and around the mouth that showed the signs of suffering. Or had it, she'd wondered, become boredom? The same amber eyes, the same dark mustache. And suddenly there she was saying to herself, while Lucien put his finger on an item in the menu—this was the tea that he would take, "You are part of all things great and quiet, my beloved," hearing the waves drawing up, retreating from the shore. Did this man know, she wondered, he was the father of her child? No, she came suddenly to her conclusion, he did not. He had no inkling of such a thing. Eleanor was talking to her now of China. "Your uncle knows *all* there is to know about China. You must see his collection of Chinese pottery. We have it in our villa at Mentone." He was, she confided, writing or was about to write a book on Chinese art. "Darling," she turned to Lucien, can't you tell Margaret something about Chinese art?" But the tea, the chocolate, little cakes and sandwiches arriving all together, she plunged rather greedily at the plate of cakes. "Do try some of these," she exclaimed, helping herself before anyone else to a large cream puff, "they are perfectly delicious. Nothing I enjoy so much as a good cream puff." Lucien meanwhile looked critically at the tea. "Little bags," he said in a voice of great disgust; nothing he deplored so much as tea in little bags. And drinking the good tea (for in spite of all the fuss he had made about it the tea smelled fragrant and delicious and she kept on wishing she had not allowed herself to be bamboozled into ordering that rich, too-heavy chocolate) he began to change his mood. Suddenly and with a jaunty self-conscious gesture he put his hand into his coat pocket and drew out the paper-covered novel she had noticed that he carried. And she might have been wrong but she imagined he was attempting to describe a little circle round the two of them as he handed her the book. "Have you read this, Margaret?" he said. No, she had not; was it good, she asked. He closed his eyes an instant as though attempting to gather up and then express if possible something of the exquisite pleasure he was still capable of snatching for himself and even in the midst of an existence spent mostly in the company of this foolish, garrulous woman. It was remarkable, in his opinion the greatest novel ever written. "But the greatest?" she'd expressed astonishment to think she'd never even heard of it. "Your Uncle Lucien is," said Eleanor, bridling a little, "a connoisseur. He knows *all* there is to know about books." "You must read it," said Lucien. "You will like it, Margaret," and he looked straight into her eyes.

She leafed through the little volume. *Du Côté de Chez Swann,* she read, making a note of it for future reference, by Marcel Proust, and the situation in which she found herself presenting her with such a staggering list of questions, it seemed to her impossible to cope with them. Had Lucien prepared this little incident in advance, placed the book in his pocket with the intention of drawing it out at exactly the right moment? Had he thought thus to tell her that after all he had a life of his own, and that this imbecile chatter was not the whole of it? Was he not somehow or other trying to tell her that he had not actually changed, that this was the same Lucien who had at one period in her life been her mentor, taught her the love of good books, developed in her that passion for poetry that had stood her all her life in such good stead? Was he not attempting to say to her in those few brief words, "You will like it, Margaret," that he and she, not he and Eleanor, were the pair who really should have spent their lives together? And was he not at the moment experiencing the most excruciating chagrin at having her see him in his role of slave to Eleanor? "'You'd *love* our house in Mentone, you simply must come some day for a visit. It's crammed with books. Lucien has a splendid library. Haven't you, darling?" Eleanor laid her hand on his arm. The twists and turns of life, the irony of the moment could hardly be rivaled. Sitting here with Lucien, with whom she had once shared the high comedy of the family scenes, their humorous observations, glancing off from Grandfather Foster to Cecilia and then back again as always to her grandmother, seeing now as she could not but see in Eleanor a creature who somehow combined the salient points of all three characters, her grandfather's extravagant good looks, his self-indulgent and naive pleasure in the good things of life, Cecilia's idiotic chatter, and what was really most appalling, knowing her grandmother loomed so large in this sensuous, powerful woman—her indomitable will to command, her eagle eye on every situation. Why, why, it was Eleanor who had known all there was to know, who had herself assisted her mother to keep Lucien in the dark about the child.

But why, she wondered, why on earth this particular meeting? At whose suggestion had that letter on the bright blue paper been sent off? How the questions came at her. She couldn't beat them off. What vistas seemed to open in her speculations. Had Lucien expressed a desire to see her before they returned to Europe, or might it not have been some extremity of boredom, a sagacious, well-calculated attempt on Eleanor's part to vary the monotony of their days—those drives and taking tea together every afternoon? After the meeting was over there'd be plenty to talk about. They could discuss it for weeks on end, and since she now felt certain Lucien had not known he was the father of her child it might well be that Eleanor, with the ability of complacent, comfortable people to forget the tragic and the painful, regarded the whole sad story as a kind of midsummer madness, and might even enjoy her chance to show them both, herself and Lucien, that she had you might say won the day.

She gave Lucien back the book and watched him put it in his pocket, almost it seemed to her with resignation, as though to shrug his shoulders—books, his library, this precious little volume, the exquisite pleasure he was still capable of extracting from literature, were his at any rate, even if he was unable to share them with anyone on earth. "But wouldn't Margaret," Eleanor insisted, "*love* our villa at Mentone." Lucien to her surprise practically took the words out of her mouth, launching out upon a lyric account of the beauties of the villa. It looked right out on the Mediterranean. "The sea comes blue and full," he said, "over the terrace wall; it floods the rooms. The Mediterranean is the sea," and he looked vaguely into the distance, "that always seems to be brimming over, full, full," he said, "full to the very brim." He half closed his eyes while Eleanor, you could see at a glance that the foolish, worldly, powerful woman was still head over heels in love with him, looked up into his face much as a mother might gaze on an odd, precocious, gifted child. She patted his arm as though to say, "Really, Margaret, isn't Lucien wonderful?"

But he relapsed presently into silence and conversation had for an instant flagged. Eleanor however, allowing only the briefest silence, transferred her touch on Lucien's arm to her own. *"Tell us,"* she exclaimed, trumping up a gush of enthusiasm, something about *yourself,* Margaret. You must be an accomplished singer by now," and she looked around the room as though expecting a grand piano and an accompanist to appear at once. "I *wish* we could hear you sing."

It had been too much for her, the questions and intimations, and such a flood of memories accompanying them, and now remembering how she used to feel in Lucien's presence, longing to do something, to smash the plates and tumblers, to throw some kind of bombshell into the midst of all that talk at the dinner table, she did literally throw her bombshell, and with a kind of fiendish, hysterical delight in watching its effect upon the two of them. No, she wasn't singing any more, she said. She thought surely they had heard she'd given up trying to be a singer. Eleanor was nonplussed. "Not singing? What *are* you doing?" And it was then she'd shot her bolt. "Why," she said, "at present I'm swamped—immersed in labor unions." Lucien put down his cup of tea. "In what?" said Eleanor. "Labor unions," she repeated. What devilish delight it gave her to pronounce the words. "I don't understand." Eleanor was obviously bewildered. There was a big strike on, she explained to them, a laundry strike. She had as a matter of fact taken the afternoon off. She should at the moment be assisting the girls on the picket line. "The what?" asked Eleanor. She reiterated the explanation, "the picket line," pronouncing the words precisely. Eleanor and Lucien exchanged an outraged glance, and she perceived at once that he had, and with appalling suddenness, as though taking cudgels up against a common peril, joined his indignation up with Eleanor's. Something indeed was going on between herself and Lucien, a kind of flashing of swords, a crossing of lances, just as though he said to her, "What, you, Margaret? Betraying your own class?" forgetting as he apparently had what in the past had been apparent to them both, that she was not, when all was said and done, and never had been exactly what you might call one of them.

The rest of that poignant little tea party had been all but intolerable. She had shocked, she had wounded, betrayed them. That was the substance of their exchange with her, and though they made an effort to recover a semblance of geniality it was difficult to get on with conversation. Life was, she kept telling herself, a business. She must not allow these little ironies to get her. They were inherent in the social comedy. Life was full of just such little incidents. A remarkable scene, she remembered thinking to herself, for a novelist. What a good novelist could make of such a situation. Why not? What was to prevent her from putting it some day into a novel? She finished her chocolate, Eleanor gobbled up the remainder of the cakes, Lucien allowed his tea to grow cold, and they did their best to turn the dreadful information off with a kind of affectionate banter, an assumption that it wasn't true, that, being as they still conceived her to be no more than a foolish misguided girl, she would presently become a more disciplined member of society and regain her sanity. And when at last they all got up to go, they accompanied her out of the dining room and through the wide hall to the door at which they'd entered. There had been the liveliest exchange of little jokes and pleasantries, and when it came to bidding them goodbye she was again enfolded in that ample bosom. The invitation was renewed, she must, the next time she came to Europe, come and make a long, long visit to them at Mentone.

And then again, the whole experience was something she had read of in a novel; not her own, oh not her own. Lucien took her hand and kissed it in his gallant European manner, and there was, believe it, she had said to herself, or not, a note of reproach in his voice, as though she had been the one to deal the mortal injury.

FOUR

Phew, Miss Sylvester ejaculated, making, she was aware, exactly the same sounds that she had made that spring evening as, turning her back on the Plaza and the park, she'd walked at a very brisk pace down Fifth Avenue, taking long deep breaths, and presently muttering to herself, "Thank God for Mary and Morton. Thank God for Felix Isaacs. Thank God for my work"; thanking God in fact for everyone and everything able to assist her in the forgetting of her past. And if, thought the old woman, on that particular night Felix Isaacs had asked her to marry him as he had on so many previous and later occasions, she thinks it very likely she would have answered, "Yes, indeed I will."

But an end to all these ifs and might-have-beens. Let it be, let it be, she said aloud. At any rate she'd walked all the way down to Ninth Street and then east to Second Avenue, and at St. Mark's Place, in front of the high iron fence that enclosed the tombstones and the old brown church she'd stopped and looked up at Mary's lighted windows, allowing herself to rest in the comfort they brought her, for Mary's apartment across the way on Tenth Street, with its spacious, high-ceilinged rooms, its charm and warmth and welcome, had been the place in New York she'd loved the most, and there had been something about it, lingering there looking into the churchyard, the chestnut trees in leaf, the shadows of the leaves and branches thrown upon the gravestones and the church, with Mary's windows glowing warm behind the boughs. It gives her back in all its fullness, thinking of it now, that brief period before the First World War when in association with a few friends and a great many people of various religions, nationalities and classes she had shared the same expectancy, as though under the ministering direction of all that hope and work and effort one might actually expect to see a better, braver world emerge. A small holding in time, she thought, for was one not at liberty to speak about an era as a home, a bit of spiritual property now demolished and which one had once regarded as one's own?

She was late, and much to her surprise and pleasure had found Felix there when she arrived. They'd sat down without her and were excitedly discussing the strike. Several young women had been arrested and, according to Mary, cruelly beaten up. One of them was she firmly believed in a critical condition. She had herself laid hold of a policeman and called him a brute and a bully, and he had struck her across the face. Why she had not been taken off in a Black Maria she wasn't able to tell. She was standing bail for all the young women, and Felix, whose knowledge had brought him in to be of help in the problems arising from the strike and the arrests, had forgotten the legal technicalities and all that difficult jargon and was together with Mary and Martin letting himself go. He was angry and excited. He wanted to get the facts before the public. He was determined to write an article and was questioning Mary, who had, the fine, intrepid creature that she was, worked all the previous summer in a big steam laundry just to see what the conditions were and was telling him about the heat, the long hours, the meager pay.

The windows were open. The smell of the chestnut trees in the churchyard together with the smell of heat-drenched pavements came drifting in. How delicious it was, this first hot summer night, sitting here in Mary's pleasant dining room with the roar and cry and rumble of the city rushing at her, experiencing this perfectly delightful sense, glancing out now and then at Second Avenue, the bright lights, the restaurants, the theaters, the bakery shops, all those Bohemians, Austrians, Hungarians crowding the pavements, that the whole of Central Europe was impinging upon her. Listening to the conversation, to the outdoor laughter, the voices, she kept saying to herself, this is real, this is my life, these are my friends.

She did not take a large part in the discussion. Every now and then she'd say "How terrible," "It's an outrage," or something of the sort. She was intent on watching Felix. He paced up and down the room, lighted one cigarette after another, questioned Mary, stopping occasionally to make a note of what she said. He was she'd thought a very extraordinary looking man. There was something about him different from most of the intellectual Jews of her acquaintance. He did not have that familiar gesture, the lifting and arresting of the arms and shoulders, assertive and at the same time repressed, as though the impulse towards emotionalism in conflict with habitual repression induced an awkwardness, a kind of bodily malaise. He had a peculiar bodily grace. Tall, blond, with that curious stiffness of the arm, throwing it out abruptly, the fingers held together, the thumb at right angles to the hand. He made her think of those figures in ancient Assyrian bas-reliefs, asymmetric, stealthy, the body under strict control. She had seen the type in the ghetto. It differed from most of her Jewish friends whose Semitism seemed to lie upon them in a more self-conscious, brooding manner, something younger about him as though he'd skipped the experience of the ghettos and the persecutions and had gone back to the youth of the race. His face was long and pale and he had a blond pointed beard and full red lips. Really what an exceptionally interesting creature he was. To marry him would be an excellent way to begin life anew, to turn her back completely on her past. She'd kept saying to herself, "Mrs. Felix Isaacs, Margaret Sylvester Isaacs." What a nice, what an extremely interesting name that would be. Or she might perhaps take up Silvestro and assert her Italian origins. Mary was always saying to her, "You're a perfect fool. What's the matter with you that you refuse to marry Felix? He's one in a million. What? You think you're too old for him? He's nearly ten years younger than you? Stuff and nonsense. You say you're not in love with him? What does that matter at your age? Think of growing old and solitary! What devotion, what friendship you will find with Felix." Watching him intently she'd thought it was perhaps those full red lips above the pointed beard, so sensuous in the ascetic face, that troubled her. Once he had lost control of himself altogether and kissed her passionately on the lips and she had recoiled at the thought of his passion. Passion had been burned right out of her, that was what stood in the way of her saying yes to Felix. But none the less, none the less, after her experience of the afternoon she must forget all that, she must lay herself open to love, to passion. Felix was, there was no doubt about it, a most attractive man.

When he'd walked home with her that night she'd hoped, contrary to her accustomed desires, that he would stop in the midst of their conversation and say as he had done so many times before, his arm thrown out stiffly, the fingers held together, the thumb at right angles with his hand, "Margaret, will you marry me? I love you deeply. I feel quite sure I can make you happy." But he had done nothing of the sort, walking west to Fifth Avenue through the soft summer night and up the avenue to Twelfth Street with that wash of cool moonlight engulfing them, he'd gone on about the laundry workers and Mary. What a remarkable woman she was. Why, when she'd worked in those laundries, he'd had it from a reliable source, not a one of those women with whom she'd been associated had so much as suspected that her background differed from their own.

"More than you ever could have done," he'd said, and at her door he'd left her quite abruptly.

She'd let herself in and walked up the two flights to her apartment, and when at last she'd got undressed and into bed there she'd lain, feeling as though she'd walked all day through a long, incredible dream. Today, she'd said, and yesterday; tomorrow. The strangeness of life had overwhelmed her, and there had been that pear tree in full bloom drenched in moonlight standing up between the clotheslines in a yard on Eleventh Street. It had seemed to her she had never seen a sight so naked, forlorn and lovely. Suddenly and to her surprise she'd found the tears were streaming down her cheeks, She'd stretched out her arms in the direction of the pear tree. "Give me back my child," she'd sobbed.

FIVE

If Felix had asked her to marry him on that night in May she would most assuredly have said yes and on the impulse of the decision and with that need upon her to shed her past she would doubtless have started off in his company the very next morning to procure the marriage license and gone with him as soon as possible to find a justice of the peace to pronounce them man and wife.

Strange are the vagaries of chance. He renewed his invitation on many other occasions, "Margaret, I love you profoundly." She could hear his voice now and see the look that used to suffuse his face, the pupils of the eyes dilated, the forehead and the cheeks noticeably flushed; his hands trembled and his voice shook. Whenever she saw him so overcome by emotion and sensed the depth of the passion she aroused in him she would invariably say to herself, no, no, I can't go through with it, and she would say—(it had become almost a formula) that she was too old for him; he should find a younger woman; and moreover, she tried to state it as gently as possible, she was not in love with him, nor did she feel inclined to fall in love with anybody. Sometimes he would cry out with undisguised bitterness that she was a cold and passionless woman.

She'd treated him abominably, taken all he had to give and given nothing in return. She must have made him suffer cruelly. It was better he used to tell her to have her on the terms she imposed than not to have her at all. And so it was that their companionship continued. It is only in looking back upon it now that she begins to realize his persistence was founded on the hope that his devotion might become so necessary to her that she would eventually change her mind. He pursued her thus for nearly twenty years and in his company she enjoyed New York in the most free, familiar and delightful fashion.

He was, like many Jews whose sense that they belong nowhere in particular makes them as much at home in one place as in another, a thoroughgoing cosmopolitan. He was determined to extract from the city in which he lived the very best it had to offer. There was a kind of arrogance in his demand for excellence. He seemed to be perfectly at home with all the arts and his response to them was sensitive and fastidious. A man untiring in civic duties, a busy lawyer, where did he come by so much knowledge of music, art and literature? Did he pluck it from the air—was it bestowed upon him at birth? she would ask him. His answer was interesting and profound. "We are born old, my dear."

Yes, that was the key to the riddle, she thought, and seemed to see her old friend again, the slender, asymmetric silhouette, the abrupt gestures, the arm thrown out stiffly, the long fingers, the long face, the pointed beard, his resemblance to some youthful figure in the old Assyrian bas-reliefs. Well, his looks belied him; he had escaped no iota of his heritage. He was born very old indeed. There were realms of his spirit which she was inclined to think she could not even imagine. He had given her a liberal education, free instruction in the arts and humanities. When they went to concerts or exhibitions together she had the curious impression that he had heard the music—seen the pictures many times before, that nothing was new to him and that he was incapable of a purely fresh response; whereas with her, dear me, exactly the opposite was the case. She had had, with him for her interpreter, a sense of seeing and hearing everything for the first time.

She and Felix enjoyed New York tremendously. To remember certain places is always to be accompanied by him—the Metropolitan Museum, Carnegie Hall, Central Park on Sunday afternoon. To think of one of those high, uncovered Fifth Avenue busses is actually to be sitting on the front seat beside him engaged in animated discussion, clinging on to her hat, the breeze in her face, the bus plunging and lurching like a spirited horse beneath them. From that vantage point on how many hot summer evenings or afternoons in spring they had viewed the city together. The sky was then uncrowded with the great midtown skyscrapers. There were no towers in air, no tiers of windows in the clouds. There was the recessional architecture and they caught glimpses of it down the side streets and the prow of the Flatiron Building pushed aside the traffic at Twenty-third Street and appeared to be sailing straight up the Avenue as they descended upon it. You had a sense that the city was growing like a giant. You had belief in it—confidence. The terror and awe that inspired you today was absent. Instead there was an excitement—expectation, a feeling which she knew she shared with Felix, almost of owning it—certainly of feeling for it some responsibility. Their firsthand knowledge of its slums lent strangely enough a special edge and sharpness to their enjoyment of its areas of pleasure and delight. To be as much at home in Hester and Elizabeth Streets as at the Metropolitan Opera House or on Fifth Avenue was somehow to feel for it a very special kind of love and devotion.

Something was in the air, some connivance with the future, a naive feeling that they were assisting personally to improve the world. God knows just what it was. She believed in what she was doing. It seemed to her that every time an Italian working girl joined a trade union there was a feather stuck in the cap of progress and reform, and when any of her Italians were out on strike there she was at strike headquarters making speeches, urging them under no consideration to turn traitor and become scabs. "Donne Italiane," she'd begin, invoking them to march breast to breast with their Italian sisters, for only in numbers was there any hope of bettering their conditions and their lives—all for one and one for all. Felix came to listen to her. He admired those speeches extravagantly. He used also to go with her into the worst of the tenements she visited—a kind of self-appointed truant officer. He assisted her in getting those miserable little slaves of industry back to their schools again. Heartbreaking were the scenes they witnessed. They wrote reports and articles. Wherever they could wax indignant, wherever they could try to "do something about it," there it seemed to them they were helping to build their city on the hill.

Take it by and large, Felix was the most interesting man she had ever known. There were many layers in him of sensibility, intellect, and emotion. She could meet him on so many different levels of experience. What they enjoyed most was dining together in a leisurely Bohemian manner. They did not then drink any of the present alcoholic favorites—generally beer or a bottle of wine. They smoked a great many cigarettes, drank a great deal of coffee and talked late into the night. They were familiar with each other's tricks of thought and conversation. That tightrope on which she'd always seemed to walk poised between humor on the one hand and tragedy on the other, treading it lightly, like a dance on air, was a line not quite discernible to him. His tragic sense of life was on a deeper level, he kept it in a compartment separate from his laughter, and what she was capable of finding extremely humorous he often relegated to the department of his grief; and this because there burned within him a deeper passion for perfection. It was humanity that troubled Felix. He could not separate his ancient tragic knowledge of the human heart from his faith in what a just society might accomplish in making men good as well as happy. His kingdom of heaven was like Christ's situated right here on earth.

There had been that night she remembers with especial poignancy when she had almost but not quite been able to break down and tell him the secret that she had kept so long. The scene comes back with all its urgency, that need to speak so strong upon her. Little Bohemia on Second Avenue, the outside door opening and shutting to let in the cold, the lights of Second Avenue bright through the windows and that little old man playing his violin standing right up in front of them; over and over the familiar waltz from Weber's "Invitation to the Dance" and that handsome boy blown in on a blast of cold air carrying a tray of violets and gardenias; Felix buying gardenias, violets, burying her face in them, "Oh, how lovely"—breathing the draft of perfume; then that conversation infused with the fragrance of the flowers. "Something about you that reminds me of a child"; the old man with the violin stepping closer, the "Invitation to the Dance" continuing; "You've never lost your sense of wonder, you respond to certain things with all the freshness of a child." And suddenly her telling him about those flowers in the woods, the fields in summer, and how she'd stood before the waves; and all the time that powerful desire to let go, to tell him everything—her love for Lucien, the birth of her child, giving him for adoption; his saying "But that is pure Wordsworth, Margaret—'moments in the being of the eternal silence'—is this enough for you?" her answering "Yes, yes, it is enough," longing all the while to come out with it, to tell him everything, but telling him instead of that experience she'd never told a soul—how once in Italy when she was trying to recover from an intolerable sorrow she had found a volume of Wordsworth on a hotel table and how she'd opened it and for the first time read the "Ode on Intimations of Immortality" and how the effect on her had been instantaneous, how the meters and the movement of that marvelous poem, like the measures of a dance had carried her straight back to childhood and to those moments of which she'd spoken, the words had been for her the declaration of a creed, they had established in her heart a faith; and there was that little man still playing the familiar tune and the ineffable smell of the flowers hovering around them and Felix laying his hand on hers— drawing her hand away quickly, fearful lest she break down and tell him everything.

There had also been that night the following August when the words "Yes, Felix, I *will* marry you" had actually been moving through her mind while he begged her so earnestly to reconsider her decision. Luchow's the night the First World War broke out in Europe—sitting by the open window, a stifling heat upon the city, newsboys shouting "Extry! Extry!" a tension in the air like waiting for a bomb to burst, Felix white and stricken. "It will be long, we'll all be in for it. People like you and me will suffer, Margaret. There will be times we'll be unable to endure it. We shouldn't be alone.

We could be a comfort to each other"; hearing the voices crying "Extry, extry," seeing his face so white and stricken and people getting up to buy the papers, coming back with them; thinking yes, he's right, we should suffer this together; but getting off (so firmly rooted in her this resistance, this feeling she could not go on with it) the same worn-out objections; she was too old; he should marry a young woman; he mustn't, he positively must not ask her again—his getting up and going out to buy a paper.

SIX

It had always seemed to her, looking back on her existence, that as far as personal history went, outward events and associations, she had had as many lives as the proverbial cat, one quite separate from the other, this epoch and that, and if she examined her experience it was always to inquire could it be possible to crowd into one human span such a shattering succession of eras and events. The incredibility of it, the accelerated speed with which changes and calamities marched on! Why, if she tried to bring any sequence to her personal story after August 1914 it got so whirled round with history that the only thing to which she could compare the process was a kind of crazy newsreel of the soul—pictures collapsing, colliding, careening madly off into time, into space— faces, personalities, voices—the Kaiser with his plume and helmet, Lloyd George, Clemenceau, soldiers of France, German soldiers, dugouts, trenches, American soldiers, Wilson with his top hat, his lady with her orchids.

As for the human side of her life in those years of the first great war, they were still so poignantly associated with Mary that to think of them was to live in them and through them all with her— standing on curbs and street corners with her, watching the young men pass. How those old tunes to which they'd marched, with their enormous emotional content, carried her back to the hour and the mood. That sense she'd had after the long waiting, the fear that war might after all not be declared, the strong conviction that *this* was a just war in which one should be willing to sacrifice one's son came surging back to her, for she too had had her personal stake in all of this—did she not also have a son of fighting age? "Over there, over there"—"It's a long way to Tipperary, it's a long way to go."

And even while that music and those words assailed her she heard again those bells that rang on that November day; she lived again through that fictitious peace, sitting there at lunch with Mary and her little grandson Matthew, the bells continuing to ring, and Mary laying down her napkin, their looking at each other, uttering the word together, "Peace," each rising from the table and running through the hall to the front of the apartment, opening the window, craning to look out; and Matthew there between them, the bells still ringing and men and women running through the street; Matthew sensing the excitement, asking questions. "Peace," they'd told him, "Matthew, it is peace"; the child seeing the people, hearing the bells, catching something of that high excitement and intensity, insisting "But I want to see it," while they turned from him to get their coats and hats and he behind them, questioning; "It's peace, Matthew," they'd insisted, running to the door, the child crying out "I want to see it, please let me see peace"; leaving him there and rushing into Twelfth Street: the weather cold and gray with occasional glimpses of the sun, not too many people yet assembled, but everyone communicating, passing the word along, running in this direction and in that, not exactly sure just where they wished to be, getting themselves to the subway and presently finding they were in Greeley Square, the big bell ringing out above the statue of Horace Greeley, the pigeons fluttering in confusion and that amazing sense they'd had of being like everybody else a vessel of joy, pouring it out incessantly, the squares, the streets, the whole town flooded with it like some high tide arising; and then that motley, disordered, spontaneous parade somehow or other set in motion, and all marching together in the direction of Fifth Avenue. Into the streets and through the streets, God knows from where, from the business sections, the residential districts, streaming out of the slums, trucks, taxis, wagons, private cars, public vehicles, and on the trucks and wagons all those improvised floats, the Kaiser set up in effigy and people dancing round him, the crowds in the streets gone mad, shouting, weeping, embracing one another, boys in uniform lifted aboard the trucks and taxis, onto the shoulders of the marching crowd, flags, trumpets, paper hats, confetti, all the paraphernalia of celebration instantly supplied, she and Mary borne along, caught up in the contagion.

The marching songs persisting, the war to end all wars presumably over, there again she was with Mary on Fifth Avenue to watch the troops pass by—the Seventy-seventh Division that had fought so gallantly in the Argonne and Mary's Martin among them. She saw dear Mary's face, the eyes closed, the tears streaming (dear Mary who was dead and little Matthew killed at Okinawa), she saw the boy erect in his brown helmet, shouldering his gun.

SEVEN

And then the astonishing years, the jazz bands, the bootleggers, the speakeasies—new morals, new behavior, new indulgences. Everyone seemed somehow to recognize that there had been betrayal. Wilson's fine phrases had turned to gall upon the lips. The world would not be made safe for democracy, but there was this knowledge hovering around the heart, that the world encroached upon it, was indeed about to enter in with its insuperable problems; a crazy spendthrift will to pleasure was abroad.

She and Felix spent a great deal of time together. They looked around them in alarm, attempting to adjust to the changes that had taken place in their own hearts as well as in the exterior scene. The restaurants on Second Avenue with their pleasant Central European charm saw them no more. They frequented the speakeasies. An inordinate need for alcohol was upon everyone.

Just to think of those speakeasies is to get back again the climate of that nervous, febrile time. There were signs and signals, a behavior to which one lent oneself without a qualm, waiting at those grilled doors (uptown the brownstone stoop, downtown the basement area) and the door opening a crack and through the crack the face, the whispers, giving the password and the door opening with the greatest caution and there you were inside the overheated and somehow oversilenced place, certain of your drink. There was all that whispering with the waiters, consulting the menu with such earnestness as though while giving the illegal orders you were making up your mind whether to have soup or antipasto, and then at last beholding with satisfaction that spread undisguised across the countenance that awful bootleg liquor as it appeared, served up in the oddest crockery, upon the table.

There was about all those dreadful cocktails, that illicit wine poured from a crockery teapot into a crockery teacup, the most peculiar effect. It gave a sharpness, an attentiveness to everything and everyone surrounding her. She seemed closed in with her guesses and intimations. It might be her fancy, probably was, but remembering it now she thinks it was about this moment that something extraordinary took place in her as though she had somehow been supplied with a new equipment of nervous feelers—picking up the messages, the intimations, the way one looked and stared, received the sudden answers, exposed oneself to insolence and to initiation.

They were a noticeable couple, Felix with his marked Semitic countenance, his rather intense way of talking, obviously in love with her and she so much older. Even the way they talked arrested attention. They were interested; they liked discussion. The young were around in those days, very conspicuous indeed, determined to squeeze to the last drop of enjoyment their suddenly acquired reputation for belonging to a lost, a desperate generation. They were alert to everything; they had their ears back like little bird dogs, listening to scraps of conversation, making their quick appraisals, requiring but a glance or two to come to their conclusions. They regarded the two of them with their straight assessing stares. You could positively hear what they were thinking—"The man's a Jew. Talks well. Where did he get the blond beard and those arresting gestures? The woman is no slouch on looks. A good-looker. Getting on in years but she's got something."

It was a curious thing but at just that time she was aware that she did have something. There were sympathies and curiosities brewing in her which in a most subtle manner flowed out and brushed the minds, the hearts of these young people and in particular went out from her to the young men. There were many influences, strong currents of repressed emotion that set afloat upon the air an intricate network of inquiries and invitations and on these tenuous lines of communication she drew the young men's glances. Stare for stare, they set up the wordless exchange. She seemed to hear them saying to her, "You've got something; give us what you've got," and from the hungers of her heart, out of the love that had never found a place to rest, the questions wandered from this young man to that as though she asked of all of them "Have you something to tell me of my son? Do his nerves resemble yours? Has he this same acuteness of perception, this awareness, quick and sharp and new and born apparently of your generation—does he frequent these places and drink himself night after night into the same state of drunken sensibility?" They were in the oddest way drinking from her wells of sympathy and not without a realization of the interest their lost condition inspired they played right up to her; they dramatized their plight.

Felix was definitely averse to these glances and exchanges. He seemed actually to think that she was carrying on some kind of airy intrigue with these charming, tipsy, rather disreputable young men. Considering how little she had ever permitted him to display his amorous inclinations his jealousy was, if these were his suspicions, understandable. It made for something of a strain between them.

There was a place in Morton Street they used to go to occasionally, Dante's Inferno, and most appropriately named it was. Goodness what a hole. Approached by dark area steps, dimly lighted, never aired, phooey how it smelt. The food was good, the drinks were cheap. It was very hushed and not too well policed. She had a preference for it because it was the hangout of a little group of young people in whom she had become specially interested. Felix objected to it strongly and on the night which she has never ceased regretting he had protested vigorously as they groped their way down those infernal stairs.

They were all of them there, the young man with the chestnut-colored hair, the young man with the dark countenance, tall, slender, distinguished, the nondescript boy with the freckled face and red hair; and there were the girls she'd seen before except that the young man with the chestnut mane had acquired a new partner. She was slight and exceedingly pretty—difficult to make out. Was she just another of those girls one saw so much around the Village, their youth already frayed, burning their candle as swiftly as possible at both ends? She obviously responded with joy and immediacy to the attentions of her young friend whose lovemaking appeared to be very explicit indeed. Charming he was if one ever saw a charming young man, easy, graceful, witty, with an air about him of having issued, like Venus from her shell, full-fledged from his lost, his desperate generation.

The group pricked up their ears and laid them back as soon as she and Felix got seated and began to talk. They listened attentively and seemed ready at any moment to break into the conversation with or without invitation. Felix was talking about

Ulysses. He didn't like it—a dangerous tendency, to reduce a novel to the stream of one man's consciousness. The Russians were for him the greatest of all the novelists. They had, he believed, exhausted the novel, drained it of about all that could be said. Weren't they the first to explore the subconscious mind, the angel country and the devil territory? They'd broken down those neat integuments, they'd let in the dark, the new dimension and managed to keep it all within the framework of a novel, a novel, mind you, he said, in which men and women play their various parts, display their characters, move around, do this and that, get something going, action, situation, denouement. But this kind of thing, no good, he said, and he threw his arm out in that abrupt arresting manner. Why, it's an association test, a matching up of literary associations. To really get it, to understand it and follow it to its source you'd have to know every book that Joyce had read, to have seen and heard everything that he had seen and heard and thought about. God, you can't make a novel out of that, the flow and eddy of the individual mind. You can't get order out of that chaos.

"Hell," said the young man with the chestnut-colored hair, and he drew out the hand which under the young girl's blouse had been caressing her pretty, slender breasts. "Why can't you? He *has* reduced it all to order."

This made just the opportunity the young people were looking for. Suddenly they were all of them shouting and Felix found himself the center of their attack. It was impossible to make out what anyone was saying, no one listening to anyone—new phrases, new names, new reputations that had got suddenly circulating in this strange postwar world where everything, even the books one read and the thoughts one had, seemed to have expanded and taken on a new dimension, were thrown vigorously about. The young man with the red hair was giving a monologue on Freud. He insisted on being heard. "Hell," he said, "wasn't it Freud who'd thrown the fat into the fire?" Felix reminded him and pretty irritably that Freud had come into the picture long after the Russians. If it hadn't been for them there might never have been a Freud. They'd started the analysis and investigation, they'd begged for this descent into Hell, or if you wished to express it according to Freud—the subconscious. Nobody appeared to listen much to him. Each of the young men seemed to be an advocate for something or for somebody. The young man with the chestnut-colored hair shouted an inquiry which brought her quickly to attention recalling that slender little volume Lucien had taken from his pocket that afternoon at the Plaza. Had his friend with the beard ever heard of Marcel Proust? *There* was a novel to put an end to all novels—the greatest novel ever written, A *la Recherche du Temps Perdu.* He waved a graceful hand and draped his arm around the pretty girl beside him. "Have to wait to finish it," he said, "still waiting for it to come off the presses. The stream," he glanced at Felix with his mocking eye, "of one man's consciousness. A *la Recherche du Temps Perdu.*" He kept repeating the title not without awareness of his fine French accent. The dark distinguished-looking boy shouted the loudest and apparently most effectually, for presently an actual conversation was under way.

She had not contributed a word to the general babel, but now that the shouts and monologues had more or less yielded to discussion she realized that the young people were expecting something from her and was uneasily aware that they had taken it for granted that she was somehow or other lined up with them, indeed that they expected her to understand the habits of their thoughts, the associations they shared and the predilections they espoused. How they could have believed this to be the case she couldn't imagine, but it was evident to her from their glances, from those curious tremors and vibrations that passed on their tenuous lines of communication, that they did. She hadn't at that time read a single one of the books about which they'd been shouting and wrangling, she'd been in no position to enter the fray, but now they were talking about a book which Felix had lent to her only a few days since. Now I shall be called upon to say something, she'd thought, remembering how she had agreed with Felix that the book was difficult—very nearly impossible to understand, and that she had shared to some extent his indignation.

The young men had conceded him the floor and he was expressing himself in no uncertain terms. "A pedant," he said, "his poem is another example of the association test—trotting out all those private incommunicable references. Who wants to be jerked around on the vehicle of one man's wandering reflections?" He turned to her. "Why don't you speak up, Margaret? You're familiar with this masterpiece." "Well," she replied, and she can never think of that answer without acute regret, "after all, Felix, it is their waste land. If these young men can find their way around in it, and it's clear enough they can, maybe we'd better back down. It's a landscape with which we are not as familiar as they—it's the world we made for them. We ought to have some respect for the disgust and grief they feel in having to inhabit it."

She can see now the gesture with which Felix summoned the waiter. Her answer had not only been ambiguous and trite, it had lacked a decent loyalty, for surely the future towards which he had worked and aspired was not, he was intimating as he paid the bill, counted out the change and tipped the waiter, this land of Eliot's poem, and if these young people wished to indulge themselves in their drunken and conspicuous sorrow that was no reason for her to imply that he didn't suffer too. It was not a world he had made and he didn't like it any better than they did, and as for this infernal hole, he seemed to be implying as he helped her on with her coat and bade goodbye to the young people, he hadn't wished to come and he did not intend to return.

It was over a fortnight before she saw him again. When he finally telephoned her his voice showed no sign of injured feeling. There was no reference to the night at Dante's save for the fact that he said "We won't go to any disreputable hole in the ground." Mori's on Bleecker Street was the place he chose.

It had been recently done over and there was an air of elegance about it, with the big spacious dining room and an open gallery above, the walls white and severe and all the appointments in excellent taste. The tables were against the wall and they sat next each other, which lends a peculiar poignancy to her memory of that night. They had cocktails and wine served here as elsewhere in crockery pots and teacups. Felix was gentle and quiet but she saw at once that he was agitated. She knew that some kind of an outburst was coming and was preparing herself for one of those painful proposals. Dear me, she'd thought, why must he keep this up for so long. He ought to know by now it's hopeless.

"Margaret," he finally began. She waited, reluctant to help him out.

"I have something to tell you," he stammered, and laying down his teacup spilled his Chianti all over the tablecloth. "I am going to be married."

It was like a blow straight between the eyes. "Oh, Felix," she exclaimed, aware that her voice expressed more consternation than delight, "I am so glad. It's what I've always wanted for you."

She placed her hand on his. "Is she young?" she inquired. "Do I know her?"

"She's not so very young," he replied, attempting to disguise his agitation. "Yes, you do know her, or at least you've seen her once or twice. You've talked to her over the telephone."

"But who is she, Felix?"

He came out with it quickly, a little defiantly. "She's my secretary, Rachel Weil."

"Oh," she exclaimed again, "oh, how nice."

"Yes, Rachel Weil, my secretary," he stammered again, grabbing his napkin and mopping up the wine. "She's been," he blurted it out painfully, "my mistress for over ten years."

Again she felt as though he'd struck her between the eyes and, it was utterly lacking in decent appreciation of what he had endured at her hands, she'd felt grieved, shocked, indignant. Felix of all people! Such infidelity from him. And there it all was written across her face as plain as day. "All these years?" she asked when she had gained her breath.

"Yes," he said, "all these years. She's a warm and passionate woman. I have asked her now to marry me."

She is certain she would not have experienced so accurately all he underwent had she not been seated so close to him. He was determined if it was humanly possible to control himself, but all the restraint she had so long imposed upon him broke down. His feeling surged up and mastered him. He put his hands before his face and succumbed to a succession of sharp, convulsive sobs. A more distressing moment it is impossible to imagine. He did his best to pretend that something he had eaten was choking him and seeing this she summoned a waiter and asked for a glass of water. "This gentleman has swallowed a fish bone," she said.

What with the commotion the little drama had stirred up, getting and gulping down the water, the waiter hitting him, vigorously on the back and each of them engaged in carrying off the pretense, it wasn't too long before Felix had himself well in hand, and presently they appeared to be conversing in the calmest possible manner.

Then there had been all that intimacy, that gentleness between them, which each had tried desperately to cling to and prolong. Her indignation had passed as swiftly as it had come and how humanly, how exquisitely Felix had understood her shame and chagrin for having felt it. It was upon that core of finesse, delicacy, and depth of feeling in him she'd rested gratefully. He had allowed her to feel that he rested and reposed on what he knew he had in all fullness and sincerity—her friendship and affection. She was concerned about everything he told her of his plans. He was moving to Washington to go into partnership with a friend. A good arrangement for him he believed and he had high hopes that his knowledge of labor relations might result in a government appointment. That was as she knew well what he had always wanted most. There was on the whole a better future for him in Washington than in New York. To this they both agreed. She kept assuring him that he was not old, that he would have a successful and a happy life. She hoped that he would have a family. Was Rachel she asked too old to bear him children? No, he said, and with the greatest earnestness, he hoped, he trusted not. They both of them desired children. And so they talked together there at Mori's until the waiters began to whisk the tablecloths off the empty tables, positively inviting them to leave.

He took her home as he had so many, many times before. They walked up Sullivan Street and crossed Washington Square. It was a pleasant April night and the spring mist hung about in the trees and shrubbery. The pavements were wet and gave off a smell of spring. There was a special smell they both agreed that hung about the Square. It was a bit too damp to sit down. They were very loath to leave a place so crowded with memories, with nostalgia for an epoch—beliefs and hopes they knew had gone past all recall.

Outside her stoop on Twelfth Street he took her hand and held it for some time. "Good night, Margaret," he said, "goodbye."

"Good night," she said, "goodbye, my dear, dear friend." And that was the last time she ever laid her eyes on Felix.

EIGHT

That feeling she had had of being somehow protected from anonymity and rootlessness suddenly gone from her heart. The long accustomed habits, calling Felix up, knowing that Mary was always at hand with her wisdom and her companionable wit, the basic reliable love still regulating the behavior of her thoughts (I must tell this to Mary—Mary would adore that, I'll call up Felix) and on the brink of all these feelings, thoughts and impulses the knowledge that she would not see her friends again and the great need to see, to hear, to have the usual talk, the old exchange.

Gone they were, vanished before she was prepared for losing them, and the shock of Mary's death the more unbearable because it might so easily have been avoided. If she had taken the train as everyone advised instead of going over those bad roads in that rattling old Ford, the day so wild and rainy; or better, if she hadn't gone at all. It had been unnecessary to attend that hearing, everyone had told her so, but determined she had been to go and in that car she so adored. Why, the moment the boy had brought the telegram and before she'd even opened it (what an uncanny thing) she'd known exactly what had happened—all day long that heaviness of heart upon her, that foreboding.

She'd been the first to get to Beacon and only just in time. Clear enough from the look on the doctor's face and the looks on the faces of the nurses that there wasn't a chance, and Mary waiting for her in that immaculate bed, whiter than the sheets that covered her, had conveyed the same intolerable message. She was conscious still and fully aware that she was dying. "Are you scared, Margaret? Well, don't be, darling. I am not," she'd whispered as though she were husbanding her strength for further conversation. She had taken her hand, but she'd been unable to utter another word. She'd closed her eyes. What could she possibly have said to Mary? Just being there with her, holding her hand while she lay dying seemed enough for both of them. The great experience had been rounded off by Mary's words. Gallant she was in her life and in her death. Beloved Mary Morton. Miss Sylvester drew a long breath as though she wished for a moment to hold her love and close it in her heart.

Life had struck at her again; but that was its behavior. It struck one blows and as far as outward events and circumstances went she seemed to have had, as she so frequently remarked, as many lives as a cat. The world which had confronted her was very feverish indeed. It invited to change and experiment—everybody running frantically about in search of distraction, and after a nearly unendurable year of trying to master her loneliness and adjust to life and its new conditions she too was caught up in the contagion. There had been that something brewing in her, God knows just what it was, she was over fifty and she discovered what honestly had come to her as a great surprise, that there was as you grew older no letting down emotionally. The hungers and thirsts increased, they struck at one with sharper thrusts. At any rate she used to regard herself in the mirror and see reflected there a not uncharming woman. Yes, she had some power to charm and to arrest attention; a gift with people. If she made an effort she could collect new friends, she could make the acquaintance of people who would interest and amuse her. New York was crammed with men and women one wanted to know and perhaps could. She might, and the idea struck her, she remembers so well one evening when she was feeling particularly bereaved, buy herself a house (real estate was a good investment). She could do it over, live in half of it and rent the other half. She might give little parties. She might make it a center for finding interesting companions—people with gifts and creative talents.

And so, and so. The heart has a way of renewing itself; life had at all times its gifts and invitations and New York at that quite dreadful moment dangled them conspicuously before the eyes—everyone spending so much money and extra dividends appearing so unexpectedly as one ruminated over one's breakfast. Why yes of course, that was exactly the thing to do—to buy a house. It would give her something to think about. A home that actually belonged to you—what could make you feel more secure and permanent? It should be west of Sixth Avenue, it must be in the Village proper. And following this decision she got to work at once to search for the new home. Accompanied by that voluble young woman from the real estate office who, armed with keys and authority to let them into houses, to knock at the doors of private apartments and as soon as they entered to begin to act as though the house, the premises and everything but the chairs and tables of the lessor were already in the hands of her client ("you can knock down a partition here, you can throw out an extension there, you can add a bathroom, excuse me, you don't mind if I open this door?"), she found herself beguilingly employed. It was exciting enough imagining herself leading so many gracious and decorative existences in so many different houses, rooms, gardens.

Finally she found on Grove Street precisely what she was after—a Victorian house, nothing especial to look at from the outside, brick with a high stoop and ornate ironwork, built probably in the eighties. It had been unnecessary for the real estate lady to tell her a word about its possibilities—she saw them at a glance. The house was constructed according to a familiar pattern and she knew its layout so exactly that directly on looking around she was able to choose her own quarters and dispose of her tenants in the most satisfactory manner. Ah, this was to be hers, she'd thought, as she entered the ground floor apartment. She'd always liked space— here she had it. The two long rooms and an extension; and ah—a garden, a pear tree. She'd knock down the partition between the two big rooms and she'd keep both fireplaces exactly as they were, marble roses and lilies and acanthus leaves intact, and between them she would run up her bookshelves (books she thought and winter—open fireplaces, flowers). Ah yes, and the extension; she'd draw all this space out towards the windows and the garden. You couldn't knock down the partitions, but you could perhaps widen the doors. Anyway she'd leave them open. There she'd sleep; there need be no visible trace of her dressing or sleeping arrangements, for on the right was a small room she could use for dressing and a bathroom leading from it; and as for the bed, well that should be magnificently disguised. There and then she saw her lovely gracious suite decorated in relation to her fine old piece of needlepoint which she would throw over the low, the comfortable divan, the walls were painted, the curtains hung, books, rugs, lampshades taking up its subtle shades and colors; furthermore, furthermore, the ugly doors would be replaced by long French windows and beyond and through them the pear tree, that spot of beauty and delight, would guide the eye of the entering visitor down the vista of the room to rest upon its shining beauty. My home! she thought, and her heart warming to it and her imagination continuing to embellish it she constructed between the extension and the second fireplace a graceful little stairway and below, white and severe and quite Italian, her dining room with open archways leading to the large, bright, pleasant kitchen—all somehow arched and aired and sunny and filled with the joy of that perennially blooming pear tree. And yes of course, oh yes of course, there were the tenants to consider. Behind the kitchen there'd be ample space (she'd put in a bathroom and kitchenette) for a small apartment at the front which she could rent to a nice neat quiet bachelor or perhaps some unobtrusive woman and upstairs the two floors which she could admirably adapt for renting. She figured out, the real estate lady assisting her, the total yearly rentals and, naturally, much exaggerating the price she'd ask the tenants and underestimating the upkeep and repairs, they added to a total sum of such splendid proportions it appeared the whole exciting venture was not only a satisfactory solution to her problems but an exceedingly sagacious investment of her money.

What a business the enterprise had been, selling securities, taking out a mortgage, searching the title and, after that, remodeling and discovering that the estimates made out with her contractor proved quite different from those she'd sketched in her imagination. She'd chosen, take it by and large, a man she liked, Mr. Kopf, a fat, genial, moonfaced creature, honest on the whole, inclined to be generous and say he'd throw in this little bit of painting or that little job of carpentry that wasn't in the contract.

But slow, mortal slow. It had all taken longer than she'd figured out. She'd been kept in town through the entire summer.

She'd enjoyed it, the walk from Twelfth Street over those sizzling sidewalks, lingering in the Square, improvising schemes about the house and meeting Mr. Kopf in Grove Street every morning, scolding him or buttering him up as the case might have been. Pleasant it was walking through the rooms she'd presently call hers, looking out the windows on that tiny plot of city property—her garden, and the summer heat casting over her tree, her garden and on the backs of all those houses, all the little gardens, its peculiar spell—some intensity about it hearing saws and hammers and the voices of the carpenters and plumbers busy in the house behind her and thinking how she'd feel at home in Grove Street.

It was autumn however before she was able to move in after plenty of brushes with Mr. Kopf, hurry and strain and nervousness. But finally in the late September days there she was inhabiting her house. To say she'd loved it was to state it mildly. What a delight to wake up on those autumn mornings with the windows open listening to those sounds, believe it or not, thought the old woman—hens, a rooster crowing, for what with all the Italians in the vicinity, Antonio's lot behind that boarding at the junction of Bleecker and Grove Street, where he kept his hens, a donkey and a horse, there'd been something almost bucolic about life in Grove Street. How she had enjoyed getting to know her neighborhood, starting out to market, the smells on Bleecker Street—cheese, oil, garlic—carrying her off and away to streets in Rome or Florence and that bright display of fruits and vegetables on the pushcarts and the stalls outside the vegetable vendors'—a veritable market garden, the lettuces and fruits so freshly watered, sidewalks wet, Italians in the crowds haggling and jabbering away in their various dialects and returning home with her market bag spilling over like an autumnal cornucopia.

She'd been loath to start the search for tenants. To complicate the pleasures of her new life with business seemed a shame, and so she put it off. Over her furnishings and final decorative touches she'd lingered as long as possible. Why she'd never been so extravagant in all her life, though to be sure she'd tried to justify every purchase with one rational explanation or another—this was the place she'd live in for the remainder of her days, and after all she was planning to entertain, to give other people a chance to enjoy her home. And so, sitting first in one chair and then in another, viewing the big room from every possible angle, she'd attempted to think out her decorator's problems. There was one thing she felt was missing. She'd known it from the moment she moved in—a grand piano. She must have a grand piano; the room cried aloud for it. Moreover it fitted in so well with her schemes for peopling her life with new acquaintances. No difficulty at all in imagining the winter nights with both the fires lighted and some young pianist playing as though he'd been inspired. Ah, she knew exactly where she'd place her instrument—there, backing on the stair rail and behind her softly lighted bedroom, the garden dark beyond.

And so, and so (it took a month before she bought it) she got her new piano. It looked as well, and even better than she'd imagined. Ah how she used to love to sit and strum upon it. She was nothing of a pianist, but what delight it gave her, lightly touching the keys and how the little tunes she played enticed the dreams. A bit melancholy they were, for there is always a touch of melancholy in the daydreams—lovely, soft and satisfying to the soul; there'd been in them fulfillment of one kind or another. And what, she would wonder as she played, was it exactly that she wanted? Perhaps to be—well, not exactly that, but something similar, a kind of patron of the arts—to have, ah well, you couldn't use that word, it sounded too pretentious, a kind of salon? No, certainly not that, but to cultivate charming creative people. She had a gift of making others easy with themselves, a gift for entertaining, getting the right kind of friends together. Felix had always told her there was the making of an artist in her. Yes, yes, she had always known it, she had an artistic temperament. Too old to be creative, but—but, there was this way she had with the young—with young men in particular; and if her life had had its bitter sorrow might it not be possible that she could draw on this bereavement? Was there not a depth, a rich fund of understanding—sympathy? Her heart was full, it was flowing over she assured herself, touching the keys, trying to remember a Chopin Prelude, a bit from one of the Beethoven sonatas; and seeing as she played, the curtains by the long French windows (they were just as she had planned them and the pear tree leafless there beyond) move lightly in the breeze that stirred them.

NINE

Flotsam and jetsam, thought the old woman, and she beat her breast, flotsam and jetsam. Those were the words, try to drive them away as she invariably did, that came to her mind whenever she thought about her basement apartment. And why should she have gone out of her way to furnish it, taking so much pains to make it resemble the boudoir of an interior decorator? If she'd left it unfurnished there would have been more permanency, the tenant would have had to bring in his bed, his desk and books and chairs and tables and after he'd hired a van and got his things transported, there would have been some obligation to pay his rent and stay. But to go out of her way to furnish a basement and in the Village in those days; why, it had been an invitation to trouble. She began to conjure with the ifs and it-might-have-beens, and again she beat her breast. If she hadn't rented the basement at all, just kept that front room for herself as she had seriously considered—a little guest suite. It was putting those friends of hers into the two floors above, giving them the duplex instead of keeping each floor a separate unit and just because they'd overpersuaded her, and asking them less than she'd planned to, and then thinking she could make up the deficit by furnishing the basement and demanding a good round sum for it.

To call it naive was mild indeed. Those discreet and careful furnishings, the pretty Chippendale desk, the expensive rug and hangings, those good prints she'd found and framed with such particular care. Ah, ah, she put her hand to her heart as though her thoughts were becoming too painful to endure. The only things that were apparently necessary in the basement apartments were the beds. Yes they needed beds. They were all that was necessary; and for her to think now of that narrow mahogany four-poster with the box mattress and the handsome spread she'd finally settled on was, she said and caught her breath, too ironic for words.

Suddenly she began to mutter to herself swift incoherent words, "My dear, my dear one," as it came back again, the excruciating story, just as she'd narrated it in her novel and feeling it here, here in her heart—memory flashing back those scenes and situations— and seeing that charming boy ("Yes, yes indeed you were, you were charming, beautiful"), letting him in herself that winter evening— the young man with the chestnut-colored hair. There he had stood, hatless and without an overcoat, throwing back his head, trying to brush the snowflakes from his shoulders, smiling, showing his fine teeth, his face responding with pleasure to the warmth and firelight as he came into the room.

It *had* been a surprise! He was a most beguiling young man, but she'd been determined under no considerations to have him dwelling in her basement floor. "Yes?" she'd inquired as coldly as possible and implying she hadn't the ghost of an idea what he was there for, just exactly as though there'd been no sign "Apartment to Rent" tied to the area rail.

"We meet again," he'd said and with that touch of impertinence that somehow or other enhanced his charm he'd taken his cigarette case from his pocket and looked around.

"Yes?" she'd repeated, not so much as offering him a chair, allowing him to stand hatless, covered with snow.

"Where's your friend?" he'd asked and he'd outlined with his thumb and forefinger the shape of Felix's beard, then he'd dropped his hand offering himself, as she had failed to do so a comfortable chair, and with the same incomparable gesture suggesting that she too might like to sit down he'd seated himself and lighted a cigarette. "Sorry your friend isn't here. He was a good talker. Something to his remarks about Joyce," he'd said, observing everything around him—the books, the bowl of roses on the desk. "A nice place," he'd vouchsafed and he might just as well have added as he took her in from head to foot "and you are, my dear lady, an extremely attractive woman. I like your gown and the sleeves showing your pretty arms. I like your dress. Gray becomes you."

Ah well, ah well. The old woman sighed and a look of infinite tenderness flitted across her face. She mustn't linger too long over that conversation. She'd recorded it, she felt sure, word for word in the manuscript. Ah, but the intimacy, the warmth of it—the two of them there in that beautiful glowing room and the snow falling so fast outside, the firelight casting shadows on the walls and ceiling and playing over his perfectly delightful countenance. "Young man," she'd kept saying to herself, "I am simply *not* going to allow you to inveigle me into giving you my basement apartment," knowing perfectly well that he knew, though they'd not so much as said a word about it, she knew what he was there for and had firmly made up her mind not to let him have the room he wanted. Plain enough to see that he was playing for time. "Give me long enough" he seemed to be saying with every word and gesture "to melt away, well, if not all your objections, at least every vestige of your resistance to my charms." There'd been a playfulness and humor about the situation which curiously enough they'd both of them enjoyed.

Finally he'd come right out with it. "Now," he'd said, "tell me, why is it you're so determined not to let me have a look at that room in the basement?"

"Oh," she'd parried, "oh, my basement?"

"Am I so objectionable?" he'd asked.

"No, no, not at all," she'd assured him. "Quite indeed the contrary." But she had already made up her mind not to rent the apartment to a young man—not to *any* young man.

And suddenly he had laughed and she had laughed. Wasn't it foolish of her then, he'd inquired, to rig up that sign and hang it on the area rail? There were plenty of young men in Greenwich Village searching for rooms—best place in the world to put them, they could come, they could go, keep whatever hours they pleased. "Why," he'd said, "you'll never be the wiser, never lose a wink of sleep."

And thereupon she'd laughed outright. "But I want a lady," she'd explained. "You wait till you see the little place. It isn't for a bachelor at all, it's for a single lady."

Well, if she was looking for Bernard Shaw's Prossie he'd said and they'd continued to laugh, why hadn't she advertised in *The Churchman* or gone to the YWCA to put in an application. "Your procedure is, my dear lady, if you'll allow me to say so, extremely naive." And so there they were laughing together. Was it at his wit or at her folly in putting up that ridiculous sign or simply the fact that he knew perfectly well that she knew she was caught. "Oh come," he'd begged her, and he'd risen, "let me take a look at the place. What possible objection can you have to a young man at work on his first novel? Is that such a disreputable occupation?"

"That depends," she'd said, bursting again into a laugh (he had a faculty of making her say the silliest things) and all at once and to her astonishment she'd seen that he was moving toward the little staircase.

"Come, let me see the flat," he'd urged.

"But that isn't the tenant's entrance," she'd reprimanded, "— the tenant can't go through my apartment, my dear young man."

"Oh, just this once," he'd begged, "I'll never do it again." Why, you might have thought she'd already rented him the place. And down they'd gone together through the dining room and into the little flat.

"Nice place you've got," he'd said, and he'd looked around, examined one of her dining-room chairs, taken a glance into the kitchen. "Pleasantest place in the Village," he'd said, following her through the door and into that neatly decorated front room.

"Quite a place," he'd looked about, and then he'd gone directly to that small four-poster, felt the mattress carefully. "Good springs," he'd said. "Comfortable bed. Expressly made for Prossie." And once more they were laughing both together (playing into her hands like that). "Well," she'd asked, "isn't that just what I've been telling you? the room, you can see it at a glance, is not for a young man."

"No, no it isn't," he'd acknowledged, "but all the same I want it. What's your top price?" He'd made it plain enough he knew she was about to soak him.

"Fifty dollars," she'd said, adding ten to the rent she'd figured on asking and as though to justify the sum opening the door to the bathroom to display the tiling, the porcelain tub and all the shining brass. "Look at this beautiful bathroom" she'd said as she'd opened another door—"Here's the kitchenette."

"Splendid!" he'd exclaimed, "a bathroom and a kitchenette! I'm game for it." He'd fixed her squarely with his eyes.

"But I'm not going to let you have it," she'd assumed the playful note, tried to be a bit coquettish. "No, my dear young man, you really can't persuade me."

Unabashed he'd gone to the bed and begun again to press the mattress and at that she'd turned, and left the room.

Gracious how glad she'd been to get out of there, to precede him through the dining room and up the stairs, talking all the way and with a feeling of defeat already taking possession of her. "You know, my dear young man, I don't intend to take you. Tell me now, what do I know about you? I've seen you round at restaurants, I expect you keep late hours and have expensive habits, most young people do."

And so there again they'd been, the two of them together in her pleasant room, fencing, bantering, somehow taking pleasure in it, the attraction they'd felt each for the other; and she remembers how she'd fancied that he somewhat resembled Byron. Well, under no consideration would she have him in her basement.

Yes, he'd said, he wrote. He was at work upon a novel. Oh he was a hard worker. He worked terrifically. It seemed his book had been begun in Paris. He hoped to finish it here in New York and afterwards return to France. Examining his mobile, interesting face she'd wondered if the lines of fatigue under the eyes, dragging the flesh down below the cheekbones, could perhaps have been occasioned by hard work—writing took it out of people. Sometimes it left upon the countenance the same kind of marks as those traced by dissipation. Well, well, whatever his habits he was irresistible and she would have to play her hand with the greatest care or there'd be no extricating herself from the net he was casting round her.

Finally he'd looked at his watch and risen briskly. It was getting late. He was due at an appointment. And hadn't he by this time persuaded her that though his sex might be against him he'd be the best of tenants. To be sure he'd beat the typewriter, but he didn't believe she'd so much as hear him do it, and he'd drawn out his checkbook. Well, she'd thought, the young man's got a checking account. That's more than some of them have. "Do you mind?" he'd asked, and he'd gone to the desk and sat down, taken out his fountain pen. "My check is good," he'd said. "Here's an advance, and if I don't pay my next month's rent just kick me out." And back he'd come with that check for fifty dollars, the ink not dried upon it. "There," he'd said and she had taken it, looked vaguely at the signature. An interesting handwriting, she had thought. Signed by Philip Ropes Jr. Why, of all things in the world. She knew the Philip Ropeses, the stuffiest, positively the stuffiest, most conventional Bostonians. Delighted she'd been in a queer way—there was something so amusing about it, that the Philip Ropeses could have had a son like this. Hard to believe it but then young people these days sprang surprises on one. She'd been on the point of saying she knew his parents but then she hadn't, she'd never liked opening those old connections.

"Good for fifty dollars, my name is good for that the first of every month," and then he'd asked with the greatest politeness for the keys.

Weak she'd been, as weak as water. "But it isn't the first of the month," she'd protested and she'd got up: she'd gone to the desk, she'd searched for the keys, found them, put the two of them on a ring and conscious that he had risen and was standing beside her she'd turned, she'd given them to him.

How earnestly he'd thanked her. The only reason he'd asked for them he'd explained was so that he could slip in without disturbing her. He intended to be, he'd assured her, as quiet as a mouse. He'd put them in his pocket, he'd smiled; he'd held out his hand and she has to this day the firmest conviction that what he'd really wanted to do was to stoop and give her an impertinent but none the less grateful kiss, for there had been warmth between them—yes, yes she is sure of it—a kind of warmth, a mutual attraction.

"But when are you coming?" she'd inquired holding his hand an instant. "When do you intend to move in?"

"Oh," he'd said, he hadn't much to bring, only his typewriter and his manuscripts, some socks and shoes and pants. He'd soon pack up, he'd be along. She could expect him almost any day. "And mind you," he'd added, going to the door, "we've made a deal: the rent is paid." Then out he'd gone, hatless into the snow.

Well, thought the old woman, why go over it when she'd just finished reading all about it? Ah but wasn't there she wondered just this difference—letting the memories give it back? There in the novel had been the words carefully arranged, scenes, situations, and she expected she had done them well: but this, she placed her hand against her breast, this flow, this going on with it. Ah she remembered how she'd waited for him to put in an appearance. She'd deposited the check, she had even called up her bank to see if it was good and wondering all the time what had delayed him. It had been almost a week.

And then, gracious what a surprise, looking out the window on that February morning and seeing, why she wasn't even sure it had been altogether a surprise—seeing him there in the area accompanied by, who in the world but the same girl he'd had with him that night that she and Felix dined at Dante's Inferno. He'd let her through the gate and off the two of them had walked together in the direction of Seventh Avenue.

Had it been indignation? What was it she had felt? To be sure there'd been nothing illegal. Why she hadn't even made him sign a lease. Just that check on Philip Ropes the bank assured her had been credited to her account. It had been, as he insisted, a deal and as for leases, you rent an apartment and unless the contrary is stipulated it is yours to do with exactly as you please. You can bring in your girl, your dog, your pet monkey. It was this knowledge she'd had that he had tricked her. Never, never in the world would she have let him come if he'd told her he was planning to bring along that girl.

Little she could do about it. There apparently they were and she'd have to say they had given her but slight annoyance. Sometimes she'd heard his typewriter but not to be sure too often. It had been this uneasy sense she'd had of it, not of him in particular but of the lives of the young, having them there in her basement documenting, as she'd felt they were, the whole irregular and spendthrift era. For of what were they not, she began to wonder, spendthrift, of youth, of time, of money? And of something else she could not so easily put her finger on.

The clicking of that area gate got strangely on her nerves. They came in at all hours and slept, she gathered, the larger part of every day. She seldom heard them stirring till after noon. Well, it was none of her business she'd tell herself. When his month was up she'd have a talk with him. Maybe she'd ask him to move. She dreaded it—encountering him again. There'd been between them a mutual desire to avoid another meeting and after all you didn't often have to meet the tenants in your basement. And when one evening she had met him emerging from his room and without the girl how blithely he had hailed her. "Hullo, Miss Sylvester," he'd cried out as though delighted to see her again. Chilly was not the word for it, the way she'd nodded to him. Why she'd not so much as spoken, just that little nod. Well, she'd registered at least her feelings towards him and glad she'd had the chance to do so. Presently she'd have the courage to ask him to get out.

Then when the month was up it had gone on just as she'd expected. They had not paid their rent. Should she go down, knock on their door and ask to speak with them or would she write a note? Cowardly enough to write and besides she had some curiosity about that room, just what they'd done to it. Well well, she'd let it go a fortnight; and then one morning about twelve A.M. she'd heard them stirring, and down with sudden resolution she had gone and knocked peremptorily upon their door. "Come in," he'd called, his voice quite blithe and casual and she'd heard a protest from the girl. She'd found the door unlocked and opened it and there he was tying his necktie, apparently preparing to go out and the girl lying on the bed smoking. Casual they both of them were, the girl not so much as getting up. "Won't you have a seat?" he'd said and then seeing there wasn't a chair in the room unencumbered by some garment or other he'd swept the girl's pajamas and bed shoes and heaven knows what else from a nearby chair and invited her again to seat herself. She'd come he knew to ask him for the rent but—but, he'd said, embracing with a gesture that untidy room, the girl on the bed, and the dire situation in which she had presumably found them—the whole irregular establishment as though it had been something for which she should by every standard of human decency have felt concern and sympathy, he'd asked her to be patient. He was at the moment waiting to get a check for a story he fully expected to sell. Just give him a week or two he'd pleaded and though he did not say "You simply cannot throw us into the street," the words were implicit in the demand and the girl lying there smoking leaving it all to him. She had not so much as looked up. Pretty she was even in her dishevelled condition. She had on a bathrobe and had not made up, but her hair which was cropped was the purest gold and seemed to fit her small head like a shining cap. The features were delicate. Yes, there was no mistaking it, the face was sensitive, a little sulky, petulant perhaps at seeing the plight in which life apparently had plunged her. But it was the face, she felt, of a gently born and gently bred young creature. Somehow it had made her heart ache—the whole situation had made her heart ache heavily. She'd wished to turn her back upon it. She'd hated to haggle with them for her rent and so, and so, she'd been quite lenient. She'd said that she would wait, but she had hinted broadly that she wished they would do their very best to find another place. "I had not been prepared for two," she'd added and she'd taken a good look at that slovenly room. They should see, she'd said, what they were doing to her pretty flat. Yes, yes, he'd agreed, they were a sloppy pair, but they'd try to mend their ways and she had to admit she'd given them no warning she was coming. Not a chance to tidy up.

So she had left. There'd been little else to do, nothing very satisfactory accomplished, she'd reflected. He'd promised to pay as soon as possible and then she had said, but weakly, weakly, that if they hadn't paid by the end of the month she would be forced to take measures to evict them. She was giving a large party on the first of April and just why she had thought it necessary to tell them that she didn't know. She hoped they would be out before that date, she'd said, rather as though she'd considered them too disreputable to be in the same house with her while she was entertaining guests. The whole thing had been sickening to her. It had made her heart ache.

And her party; well, what could she say about that party but that it had been the most beautiful occasion? Something extraordinary had occurred, an event—moments passing one into the other, little tableaus of the heart, the desires, the dream images coming suddenly to life, and there in the midst of them she'd been, in them but outside of them, the genius in fact that had conjured them into being and looking around her, saying to herself "Can this actually be true? Have I pulled it off?" Why, it had been exactly what she'd wanted, the evening soft and springlike, the windows open and the fires lighted and all those flowers, yellow, white, pale ivory, and amber. She could see and smell them, daffodils, freesia, white hyacinths, narcissus, Easter lilies, all the Easter constellations clustered and assembled there in her room—her home.

Her dress too had been quite perfect, pale ivory and amber with a touch of young spring green and as she'd walked about she'd had that curious feeling of unreality—the compliments and the perfection. And she had managed to procure what had been the very core of her ambitions, a string quartet, one of the very best in town—there had been music with the fires lighted and all her guests responding to the magic just as she would have wished to have them. Ah, unforgettable, forever unforgettable the "Heiliger Dankgesang" in the Beethoven 132. That music, what was it, she had asked herself, occurring in her heart, feeling it climb, ascending to what celestial heights she did not need to ask, but let it climb, let it continue climbing, let the clouds burst and the effulgence stream behind the breaking clouds while she experienced such joy as never was or could be quite imagined, running as she seemed to be backward into childhood with that music, with those intimations and the remembrance of that day in Siena when she'd found and read the incomparable Ode, and being there again in that grove in Brookline picking those spring flowers, being in the summer fields above the ocean, a part of that great dance of life. And from whence came such music, she had asked herself, from what fount of knowledge and intuition, yielding herself up to it, letting the heart climb higher, higher, and saying to Felix yes, it is enough, it is sufficient.

After that was over, the spell had been cast, shed on all the guests, and she had walked through the rest of the party treading it had seemed to her upon celestial clouds, the pleasantest compliments in her ears and that delicious sense that everything was going as she'd planned. She'd had in a man to serve and a caterer had furnished the refreshments and with her own Daphne Jordan assisting everything went on without a hitch. Champagne, she had thought, looking at her guests, at the daffodils, the freesia, the narcissus—the perfect wine for such a night as this and she had lifted her glass to drink, as someone had suggested, to the spring and there at her side the young cellist who had played, it was the only word for it, like an angel, and she had told him that his performance was perfection and he had bowed and said "My dear lady, it was because you were there with that expression on your face that I performed so well." A lovely compliment she had thought carrying it with her through the evening while this little tableau melted into the next and the whole airy, fairy dream went floating away from her until the last guest had gone and there she'd been alone in her big room thinking of it all with such extreme delight.

And then because she must find somebody to talk to she'd gone downstairs in search of Daphne Jordan and found her stacking up the dishes on the dining table just as she had ordered, tired, considerate, and more than a trifle tipsy, what with all the glasses she'd emptied. Her lady must sit down and have a cup of coffee for she hadn't, she'd reminded her, had a bite to eat. "Now there," she'd said, returning with salad, sandwiches, and coffee, "eat, my lady, eat them sandwiches," and back she'd gone into her kitchen to finish with the dishes.

Glad enough she'd been of something to sustain her. Pitching into the sandwiches and salad, trying to gather and assemble the various fragments of that lovely dream her party, which for once in a way had been so completely successful, and becoming suddenly aware that something was going on in the front room she'd felt annoyance, irritation. Why should those two young people disturb this mood of happiness and satisfaction with their ugly quarrels? They were in the midst of a regular fracas. She'd not wanted to listen to them, but as a matter of fact she had done so; she'd listened attentively. She could hear them plainly, for they'd raised their voices and oh, she wished they would not use all those ugly words, throwing them at each other like that, words only associated in her mind with certain passages of the Bible and in the mouths of these young people revolting, revolting. The girl was apparently weeping and what was she telling the young man? That she was going to have a baby. Oh God, oh God, she couldn't bear it, and she'd put her hands before her face. "All right," he'd said, "you're going to have a baby. All right, that's your responsibility. No reason at all for me to believe it's mine." At this the girl had shrieked hysterically. It seemed that she was on the bed. She could hear her moving about and the springs creaking. "But Philip, you liar, you bastard, you know there's nobody but you." "How do I know it?" he'd shouted back and he had called her one of those names it had seemed to her she could not tolerate upon his lips and all the while she'd been aware that Daphne Jordan was just behind her listening at the kitchen door. She wanted to command her to go away, but then how could she? The young man was banging about, opening and shutting doors, bureau drawers, making a big racket and the girl continuing to shriek at him. "God knows, I'm crazy about you." "Shut up," he'd roared at her. "I'm getting out," and then the girl must have got up from the bed, for they were having an actual physical tussle. "Philip," she'd shrieked, "you bastard," just pelting him with the dreadful word, and there was a great sound of slaps and blows. Maybe she was slapping him, maybe he was hitting her. And then suddenly it seemed that it was over and Philip was talking in a slow thick voice while Daphne listened there behind her, mumbling this and that, and while it seemed to her her blood congealed, her heart stopped beating. "All right," he'd said, "I am a bastard, and the son of a bastard and the offspring"—he'd used the word which had turned her heart to stone, maybe sitting down on the bed or on a chair, for what she'd needed was to get a physical picture of him. What she'd needed was to have him there, folded in her arms, longing so desperately to rush through that closed door and claim his love and his foregiveness and the word piercing her heart as though he'd aimed an arrow at it, hearing him brutally, rather drunkenly, but obviously with some need upon him to redeem, to excuse himself, telling the girl the secret she had kept so long, how he'd been abandoned by his mother in Fiesole, sold as he'd put it to save her precious chastity. Then their voices growing lower, the anger diminishing, she'd been unable to hear much of what they said. But certainly the quarreling was over, mostly she heard the girl's voice declaring that she loved him. "Philip, Philip," she kept saying, and she was crying still and there had been kisses and then again the shutting and the opening of doors and bureau drawers and both of them, it dawned upon her, packing up, preparing to get out.

And there she'd sat at that table with all those stacked-up dishes round her, but frozen, paralyzed, wanting, oh desperately, to get up and rush through that door and not even knowing if Daphne was still standing there behind her. Only scraps of words and phrases and all to be put together, pieced out by her imagination, "not paying the old lady," "running out on her," "getting out of here." Had she heard something about Europe, Paris, about the story that had been accepted? Maybe, perhaps she'd made it up. There she had sat and listened and finally she had heard the door stealthily opening and then feet as cautious as a pair of thieves, the boards creaking in the basement hallway, the opening of the outer door; then faint but audible the latching of the area gate behind them.

TEN

Miss Sylvester regarded her little patch of view. She had never been able to accustom herself to it and tonight it was of such transcendent beauty, the air, the sky so clear and that small slice of a moon sailing past the tower, the stars quivering, this astonishing array of windows building up before her eyes their citadels of crystal light. Strange it should have been her portion to look out on such a spectacle as this. Strange to have lived on earth through these last eighty years. And an altogether extraordinary business writing her book, laying it away unopened and then rereading it today, sitting here turning the pages as one might turn the pages of anybody's novel, all the while reliving it, giving it back to memory, to that stream that still continued flowing. It was, she thought, looking out upon the moon, the stars, and all the glittering windows, as though they challenged her, something of a cheat—a cheat, the cutting her story off, rounding it to a finish with all that tragedy and melodrama in the basement.

Life carried on and that knowledge to which she'd been so brutally exposed became as time went on an item of familiar baggage in her heart. How long had she stayed on in Grove Street, three years or four? She wasn't sure, and the year she'd sold the house and moved to that comfortable place in Eighth Street would probably remain uncertain were it not for the fact that luck had been involved, getting out before the crash, selling the house at a good profit and making all those arrangements about the legacy, the settlement of seventy thousand dollars on the grandchild she'd never seen, completed in the spring of that same year, the funds invested soundly, capital and accruing interest to be paid at his majority and all achieved without so much as breaking that agreement never to reveal herself either to her son or to his issue.

And the years that followed her moving out of Grove Street, goodness gracious, more than twenty of them. What with the world events that rushed upon her out of the headlines, off the celluloid, out of the air, collapsing, colliding, careening madly off into time and space, how could she possibly keep track of them? After the crash that period of depression, queues of the unemployed and that soup kitchen right around the corner on Green Street, never emerging from her door without the sight of hungry men. Then there had been Hitler and all the terrifying rumors (just when had she first heard of Hitler?), then Roosevelt and the moratorium, the first inaugural speech, that voice in which you somehow trusted, then suddenly the rolling of the beer barrels so jolly in the midst of all that apprehension, and behold the bars, the mirrors, bottles, the ladies with their glasses, and all the time the rumors growing louder—youth movements, storm troopers, Jews in liquidation, windows broken in Berlin, shops raided in Vienna, the burning of the Reichstag.

How many years since she'd divested herself of her personal possessions and moved into this singularly impersonal room and here, confronted with her lone estate, resolved to write her little story, to sit down every single day and try to tell the secret she had kept throughout the years? Was it the anonymity of her life against which she'd rebelled? One had a right to one's personal history; if one had experienced strong emotion, endured one's special brand of agony, one was entitled to express it. At any rate with all the *Schrecklichkeit* that marched upon the world—Hitler entering Vienna, rolling across the bridge with all that show of military might, Czechoslovakia, Munich, Berchtesgaden, Chamberlain stepping from his plane carrying his scroll and his umbrella—switching on the radio, sallying forth to see the newsreels, how determined she had been to stick to her resolve. Why, it had obsessed her utterly. All the rumors from the air, that sense that everybody had of waiting on some dread, calamitous, unprecedented moment had not been able to deter her. Desperately she'd stuck right at it, working each and every day. It had, she is free to confess it, almost killed her, but when the spring arrived, exceptionally soft and lovely, she'd felt on certain days a curious joy, as though her heart had been assuaged, her spirit given wings to soar, to mount. There, spread upon the Flushing marshes was the great World's Fair—the fountains and the palaces of peace, and she had walked among them in the warm spring weather, an old, old woman in her declining years with something slowly growing, taking shape within her.

The King and Queen had visited the Fair, had eaten frankfurters with Mrs. Roosevelt and returned to England safely. Finally in August that cloud that hung above the world exploded, burst asunder—Poland invaded, England, France at war with Germany, Warsaw bombed, the whole world waiting for Paris and London to be strafed from the air. During the long winter of the phony war with what dogged perseverance she had labored at her task. She could bring no order, no organization to her work, it simply fell to pieces in her mind. Up and down the floor she'd paced telling herself she was the greatest fool alive. Then out of that dead calm, ah God, with what swiftness came those bolts of lightning, Norway invaded, the overrunning of Denmark, the occupation of Belgium, the overrunning of France, Sedan, the fall of France, and the miraculous Dunkirk; then a pause before the crisis and finally, staged forever on the screen of air and sky, the battle of Britain, all those nightly bombings, conflagrations, the show put on for everyone to see—that English bravery, with Churchill looming like Colossus, and all America invited to stay at home and listen to those cheerful voices of the bombed-out people in their shelters, jovial as though assembled at some pleasant nightclub, London every day in flames at all the movie theaters, and there she'd stayed to watch it, with her novel weaving through the holocaust and the horror.

After that to cap the climax Rudolf Hess flying to Scotland, and then to cap all climaxes and all surprises Hitler invading Russia, nothing to think about but Russia, those place names tolling in the mind like dirges, Kiev, Smolensk, Nizhni Novgorod. Would they hold, had they fallen? That meeting—Churchill shaking hands with Roosevelt aboard the battleship, the Atlantic Charter. And on a Sunday, the seventh of December, breaking through the music. Was it a prank by Orson Welles—a jamming of the radio? Pearl Harbor. Where exactly was it? What did it mean? Were we at war, lined up against the Axis, in it with out allies to the finish?

Disaster falling on disaster, Wake Island, Bataan, the stand at Corregidor, the sinking of the English ships, Hong Kong, Singapore, the Malay Peninsula, the Dutch East Indies; and presently the celluloid offering the eyes the visual images, the far-flung lines of battle, that wilderness of snow in Russia, the armies fighting in the snow, the cities holding—Moscow, Leningrad, and in the spring those corpses on the leafless trees in the demolished hamlets, convoys in the Atlantic, sinkings, aircraft carriers in the Pacific, dogfights in the waste of sky and ocean, landing craft, soldiers disembarking on the lonely beaches, battles in the jungles, flaming tanks, the boys arrayed in leaves and branches, with Mickey Mouse and Donald Duck and Popeye running in and out of Armageddon—sitting in that macabre twilight, wondering if she had the courage to complete her novel, Alamein, Guadalcanal, Roosevelt and Churchill at Casablanca, our landings in North Africa, and Stalingrad, the bleak, the desolated city, Eniwetok, Tarawa, Okinawa, Truk, Stalin under the palms with Roosevelt and Churchill.

And then again the voices, the announcements, sitting beside the radio—the channel safely crossed, the epic beachheads, Caen and the channel ports. And in the summer, voices that announced the Russian conquests, cities taken back, that gathering sense of safety, victory approaching, the Battle of the Bulge and hopes set back at Christmas, confidence restored, that softening up, the ceaseless strafing of the German cities, our armies on the march, the crossing of the Rhine (victory so close that you could touch it), Stalin, Churchill, Roosevelt at Yalta (the black cape, the skeletal face)—peace and the spring approaching. Suddenly that voice that struck out like a blow—Roosevelt dead at Warm Springs, the funeral train (lilacs in the door-yard blooming), the crowds at stations weeping. Then spring with all the blossoms; peace in Europe long awaited. And summer with the victories in the Pacific, the Philippines regained, the islands hopped. Truman in conference with Attlee. Truman's announcement on the sixth of August, those words reverberating round the world. Alamogordo, Hiroshima.

Nagasaki; peace.

Peace, repeated the old woman, peace, and remembering the news that she had read that morning, said aloud, or thought that she had said it, "What is man that Thou art mindful of him, and the son of man that Thou visitest him?" and she attempted to get up, for she was late and Adam waiting for her (dear me, dear me, how much money had he said he wanted? She must go to her desk and get it. Fifty dollars was the sum? No, no, she would not leave her manuscript to Adam, she would destroy it when she returned from dining. Plenty of novels in the world already. She had had the experience of writing it—that was sufficient, quite sufficient) and had she risen to her feet, had someone dealt her a stupendous blow and was it Nanny at her elbow urging her, "Yes, now, take another step, the money's in the desk, go there and get it," or was it the august angel with his hand upon her shoulder?

She fell, her head escaping by the fraction of an inch the corner of the desk and there she lay stretched out upon the carpet while the telephone upon the table by her bed began to ring, continued ringing.

And Adam who was mad and standing in the booth at the Armenian restaurant cursed roundly. "Damn the old woman, damn Mol," he said, banging the receiver onto the hook and then as he heard the coin click in the cup beneath the telephone, he pocketed his last remaining nickel and went back into the dining room to wait for his old lady, under the impression that she was on her way.